Her Favorite Cowboy

Her Favorite Cowboy

A Watson Brother Romance

ANN B. HARRISON

TULE
PUBLISHING

Chapter One

TYSON WATSON TOOK another sip of his whiskey, immune to the fire burning down his throat. After the first two glasses, the numbness had set in and he could have just as easily been sculling water for all the good the liquor was doing for him. He stared at the bottle, somehow blaming it for the foul mood he was in and then tried to focus on what he was doing.

Wife wanted, no frills or fancy ideas. Must be willing to live in the country, help on the ranch, and not be afraid of commitment.

Commitment. Such a damning word. It burned a path across the top of his head, wrapping its tentacles down the cortex of his brain, giving an extra squeeze to piss him off. Layla Cox, Queen of Independence, scared shitless of commitment. At least with him anyway. Tyson took another swig of whiskey and cursed. Damn her to hell. Got him wound up in knots over her, used him as a sex object for the weekend when she attended Rory and Gina's wedding to scratch an itch, and then... nothing. Absolutely fucking nothing!

He was punching above his weight the moment he laid eyes on her. Made sense to him even if his brothers tried to convince him otherwise. Hell, just look at him. Poor cowboy with a rundown ranch and little prospect of it getting any better any time soon and then take a look at Layla Cox. The high-powered big city lawyer who screamed sophistication and dripped money from every pore of her perfectly smooth skin.

Oh, they were good in bed together. So good they only surfaced for food and drink in the two days she'd been back in Marietta. What a diversion that must have been for her, a far cry from the normal soirees she attended with the city's high and mighty movers and shakers. Such a change from the suits she probably dated. How slumming with him must have been an eye-opener for her.

Tyson in his Sunday best clothing. A pair of jeans without a rip in them, a hand-me-down white shirt from Chance and Tyson's best hat. At least his boots had scrubbed up with a lick of shoe polish. God knew he couldn't have afforded another pair. Not until he got this horse trail riding business underway and then most of the profits, if any, would go back into the ranch. He could live with things the way they were.

And that was how he knew Layla would never be the one for him. He'd seen photos of her apartment on her flash big iPhone. All white and beige and clinical-looking. Just as well he hadn't seen them before he brought her to his bed. He'd have died of embarrassment. The gold and brown shag pile carpet in his shack, flattened in most places, worn though to the floorboards in others, was so far removed from her apartment's almost white carpet that he cringed even now thinking about it.

He glanced through the bedroom door and stared bleary-eyed at the rumpled sheets on the permanently unmade bed. It'd been hard to strip them off to wash after that weekend, but only because he didn't want to lose the scent of her when he crawled into at night, waiting for the phone to ring, knowing it was all a dream.

"You tried, boy. You gave her everything you could and she left with a smile on her face but no promises." Saying the words out loud only added to the helplessness that had tormented him since she'd waved, climbed into the taxi, and hurried back to her life. He slammed the glass down on the table and stared at the muted television screen.

Tyson blinked, rubbed his hand across his face, the beginnings of a headache already creeping in. He was so tired and lonely. It was the lonely bit that got him the most.

He stared at the notepad and the advertisement he'd started to write. Chance had dug Tyson in the ribs, told him to either contact Layla or get over it and move on, find a wife, and settle down. He'd even reminded him how successful all of his brothers had been finding mail-order brides. Chance and his Aussie wife Callie were blissfully happy, living up the road on their own ranch. Rory and Gina had made a snug family home out of the rundown house over the hill. Even the doctor in the family, Evan, had come home and found love in a not so romantic chain of events.

So why did Tyson have to be the only one trying to do things the old-fashioned way? "Go and write an ad," said Chance. "What harm could it do? You might get lucky." As if! Tyson picked up the pen and clicked it a few times, trying to come up with a witty ending. Mustn't be too city-orientated. *No, that didn't sound right.* Must like animals. *Obvious, you idiot, if she's going to live on a ranch.* Must phone back after a date.

He threw the pen down, picked up the glass, and drained it. This wasn't working for him. He grabbed the page, ripped it from the notebook and stalked into the kitchen, the almost empty bottle tucked under his arm. With angry movements, he stashed the bottle under the kitchen sink, left the glass on the counter, and turned to the phone hanging on the wall beside a pegboard. "Ring why don't you?"

Tyson took a thumbtack and jammed the paper on the board, glared at it for a few seconds, and then turned off the light before stumbling to bed.

"HELLO."

"Good morning, Layla." Chance's honey voice boomed over the phone. "How are you?"

"Great, you and Callie?" *And Tyson, tell me how he is. Does he miss me? Has he even mentioned my name?*

"She's fine. Loving life as usual. Listen, can I get personal?" His voice quieted.

"Sure. Ask away. Not like I don't owe you a few favors myself."

"Are you and Tyson heading anywhere or was it all a flash in the pan?"

She sucked in a breath, the pain of the question hitting her hard. If she had her way they'd be a couple by now but it would seem he had other ideas. "No. Merely an infatuation. I got over it once I got back to the city." *Because he doesn't care and it will never work out between us!*

"That's okay then. You see, I have a favor to ask you and I had to make sure there was nothing between you before I did it because it would be awkward otherwise."

"No problem. Now you have me intrigued. What's going on?"

"It's Tyson. He wrote this ad for a wife." He laughed. "Seems I finally got through to him. Went down to pay him for a couple of horses he put my way and found it on his pegboard."

Layla sucked in a breath, her chest constricting painfully and she pressed a hand to her breastbone. She closed her eyes and tried to keep her emotions in check but it wasn't going to be easy. Her heart pounded and her ears rang.

"Layla, are you there?" Chance's voice broke through the

fog that had settled around her brain.

She licked her lips, desperate for moisture before she spoke. "Yes, sorry. Something distracted me. Say that again."

"Tyson has written an ad for a wife and I know I'm playing big brother here but I was kind of hoping you could deal with it."

"What do you mean, deal with it?" Cold sweat broke out on her forehead and she raised a trembling hand to her cheek. Surely this ranked high up in the 'you're asking too much' stakes?

"Well, I guess what I was hoping was that you could vet the replies so he doesn't get ripped off. You know what a soft touch he is. Last thing I want is for him to get hurt." He cleared his throat. "The thing is, he's likely to take the first woman that answers the way he is right now."

"What do you mean, the way he is right now?" *I hope he's lost the ability to speak, is what I hope. Then he won't be able to sweet-talk any prospective brides like he sweet-talked me between the sheets and leave them waiting for the call that never comes.* A sob rose in her throat.

"Hey, you sure you're okay? Sounds like you're a bit emotional."

"No. No, no. I'm fine, a bit tired after a huge case but you know me. I love the fight, especially when I win big." She lifted her hand and coughed. "It was a late night of celebration, far too late for the early start I had." Actually, it was a late night vomiting over the damn toilet bowl with food poisoning from a lunch meeting but he didn't need to know that. "So what do you mean, the way he is now?"

"He's been like a bear with a sore head and he's taken to drinking more than usual. I think seeing the three of us so happy has made him question his lot in life. I think he's doing the right thing, though. He needs someone; we all do."

"And you want me to pick that 'one' for him?" *How could life be so damned cruel?*

"Look, I know this sounds bad since you and he, you know…"

"Spent a couple of days in bed? Come on, Chance, as if you haven't been in the same position, excuse my pun, and never looked at her again. This is life, we have affairs. I get that. But, moving on, you want me to vet the prospective Mrs. Watson for you?" Layla bit back the rest of the words she wanted to spit out, lest she sounded like a shrew who lost out.

"Yeah. We go way back and I trust you. Would you mind?"

"Yes and no. It feels a bit weird but if that's what you want. Are you sure he wrote it? This isn't something you and Rory hatched between yourselves to get back at him for all the years of being a gossiper are you?" After all of Tyson's snipes at Chance and Rory having mail-order brides, he was the last person she expected to do the same.

"I wouldn't lie to you, Layla. He wrote it, I promise. I'll

scan it and email it to you later today and you can see for yourself. And if you could be a little bit circumspect about which papers you place the ad, I'd appreciate it."

Really? "You want me to place the ad too and filter the replies before sending them on to Tyson?"

"Uh. Yeah. Please, if it's not too much trouble." Now he sounded unsure.

"I guess. Leave it with me then. I'll get back to you when I have something to report." She hung up before he could say anything else.

Barely holding it together, Layla pushed her chair from her desk and stood up. The view from her office never failed to thrill her. Today it made her feel ill and she staggered over to the couch and lay down, kicking off her killer shoes and tucking her feet up.

"Why is he doing this? We could have been so good together?"

Chapter Two

TWO WEEKS LATER, Layla picked up the phone and called Chance. "Chance, hi."

"Layla, any news for me? Have you found Tyson the perfect wife already?"

"Uh, no I haven't had any replies that I'd consider appropriate yet. I do have some news but it's not really anything I would discuss over the phone. I wonder if I can talk to you face-to-face?"

This was personal but Chance was the one person Layla could count on to help her in her time of need. She leaned back in her chair and closed her eyes, tried and failed to unsee the test kit in her top drawer. Her usual professional mask slipped and she swallowed, doing her best to get a grip on the current situation. She had to deal with this in her normal straightforward, no-nonsense manner if she was going to get through it. Especially since she was in the throes of finding his youngest brother and the father of her unborn baby, a wife.

"Can I come and stay with you guys for a couple of days?

I have some things to sort out in town and I don't really fancy staying in a hotel. Too impersonal if you know what I mean and I'd really like to talk something over with you and Callie. I need a solid, reliable friend to use as a sounding board." *Please say yes, please.*

"Everything alright, Layla? Not like you to be asking me for help although I hope you know that I'd do anything for you. Normally, you're the cool, calm, and collected one bailing me out of whatever crap I'm in. At least that's how it used to be before I became a staid, old married man." His concern over the phone reminded her what a good friend he was.

Their relationship had started out as purely business with the company she worked for looking over his rodeo contracts and things had gone from there. She gave him advice on more than business and Layla would be the first to admit she'd saved his ass more than once. It was time for him to repay the debt.

"Nothing I can't handle. Thanks, Chance. I'll let you know more when I can. Still have to arrange things this end then I can get a few days out of here." She said goodbye and put the phone down, clicked her nails on the glass tabletop and closed her eyes. *Breathe, just breathe.* She could get through this, she could. Thing was, it blew her mind because she was no longer in control of what was going on. Tyson had fixed that well and good for her and she didn't know whether to hit him or thank him. After all, she never put up much of a fight where he was concerned.

Layla didn't understand the hold he had over her. For one, he wasn't her type at all. A cute as all out cowboy was never her idea of the perfect man. He wouldn't fit into her world any more than she'd fit into his. At least that was the train of thought chugging through her confused mind along with the fact that he was searching for a wife and it wasn't in her direction.

Layla gave herself a moment to bring up his image in her mind, not that he was very far away from her thoughts. Especially since his brother Rory's wedding anyway. He'd looked so damned handsome in his best jeans and shirt. The little string leather tie with the silver and blue horse's head toggle, his cream colored Stetson, and the natural swagger had her before she could blink.

But it had been like that from the first moment she'd laid eyes on him. The brother of her favorite client – clients actually, if she counted the work she did for Rory and Gina in the custody battle with Fisher's grandparents—had intrigued her from the start. Every time she'd gone out to visit in their hometown, Marietta, Montana, he'd managed to get under her skin and she hadn't complained. He was handsome, devastatingly cute in his own unassuming way, the odd one out in the family and Layla couldn't figure it out. She'd never been attracted to anyone remotely like Tyson. He was a cowboy, a down and quite happy at home in the stockyards man who worked with horses and cows getting his hands dirty.

She was a city lawyer who didn't believe in going out to collect her mail without dressing in a designer suit with her hair and makeup done. They were too different, from opposite sides of the track – hell opposite sides of the world if she was being truthful. She'd attended a prestigious girl's college and a Swiss finishing school, and he'd gone to a community college and dropped out to work on a ranch. She lived in a swish white-on-white city apartment in a sought after area of Denver and Tyson lived in a ramshackle old ranch house in Marietta, boasting a leaking roof and a sagging front porch with kitchen appliances that had her shivering just thinking about them.

But she couldn't deny the attraction between them and giving herself over to the moment, or the champagne, had taken him back to his place after the wedding and spent the next two days in bed making love to him. It was the best weekend she'd ever had, the only time she'd felt truly alive apart from her first day in the courtroom. There was something to be said for the opposites attract theory. As different as they and their backgrounds were, it was the only place she wanted to be right now no matter that her brain was telling her different.

The thing was, Tyson didn't want her. He wanted a mail-order bride who wasn't scared of commitment. It would seem she didn't fit the bill.

Now was the time to find out for sure and Layla would

do it in her usual fashion. Breeze in, suss out the lay of the land, decide whether or not to make an offer of some sort and see if he took it. Layla didn't do failure well on any level. Not in her business life, not in her personal life, so she hoped Tyson was agreeable to her idea.

Layla reached over and grabbed a tissue from the coffee table. She stood up and blew her nose, gathered her thoughts. Her computer stared at her from the desk, the screen arrogantly showing businesses for sale in Marietta, Montana, home of the Watson boys and also home of the Lidderback Family Law firm, currently for sale on the main street. She mused for a moment, stood up, strode over to her desk, picked up the phone, and dialed.

TYSON DODGED THE quick as lightning back hoof of the paint horse currently having a temper tantrum. "Damn you, Shilo. I'm going to send you to the glue factory if you don't get your attitude sorted out." He grabbed hold of the halter and pulled on it, getting the horse's attention. "You'll be no good to me if you keep this up and there's no room here for a horse that can't earn its own keep, you hear me?"

"Don't know about the horse but I could hear you yelling clear down to the house. Problem, little brother?" Chance wandered over and ran his hand over the rump of the horse in question.

It lifted its leg as if to kick and rolled its eyes, ready to launch another attack. Chance ran his hand up its back and over its neck before taking the lead rope from Tyson. When he had control, he leaned in and rubbed his cheek against the horse, whispering nonsense to it until it calmed down.

"Stupid animal is all over the place this morning. Don't know what I'm going to do with him if he keeps up this kind of carry on." Tyson stood back and glared as his brother.

The horse sniffed his shirt and they bonded with each other much to Tyson's disgust.

"You could probably send him to me but I think if you stood back and took a look at yourself you'd find out what his problem is."

Chance turned to look at him and Tyson kicked at the ground, feigning ignorance. "Don't know what you mean." He looked away, taking in the beautiful view of Copper Mountain, knowing Chance would be able to read his face as he'd always done.

"You've been like a bear with a winter hangover since the wedding. What the heck's got into you anyway?"

Tyson glanced at his eldest brother and got caught in the hypnotic stare. The tension in his shoulders ratcheted up a notch and he looked away from his all-knowing, all-seeing brother.

"Bullshit."

Chance raised an eyebrow, calling Tyson out on it.

"Mind your own business, Chance. Haven't you got

something you could be doing on your own ranch without coming over here and annoying the heck out of me?"

"Probably but I had something to pass on I thought might interest you. I can leave it though for another day considering you seem to be in such an unsociable mood." He handed the lead rope over and with a wink and a tip of his hat, he walked away.

Tyson's interest piqued. "Don't be a smart ass. What's going on?" Chance kept walking, ignoring him. The horse snorted as if it was enjoying the joke at his owner's expense before putting its head down and nibbling at the grass on the fence line. Tyson dropped the rope casually around the top fence rail and ran after his brother, grabbing him on the shoulder before he got to his truck, swinging him around. The grin on Chance's face told Tyson he was expecting to be stopped. Right, real smart ass!

"Really want to know, huh?" Chance dipped his hat to shade his eyes from the sun but that didn't stop the sparkle or the knowing smile.

"Spill it."

Chance shuffled his feet in the dirt and casually draped his hands on his hips while Tyson sweated for information. "Well now, seems Layla is coming down to visit soon. She asked if she could come and stay with us, said it was personal, whatever that means." Chance turned away and walked toward his truck. He leaned back on the fender, a sly grin on his face as Tyson took in the information.

Tyson's gut clenched. She was coming back to town? Not one phone call since the wedding and their weekend together and she was on her way back without letting him know. What the hell was he going to do? The image of her naked body in his rumpled bed flashed through his mind. To be honest, the image had never left him, unlike the woman herself.

It'd been too much to hope that she would want to keep in touch with him. Once the glow of the weekend had worn off, Tyson had felt used and it wasn't a pretty feeling. Never one to give his heart to a woman too soon, he'd been ready to offer it to Layla Cox on a plate.

"Like that, don't you. Tell me what's been bothering you, Tyson." He slung a friendly arm across his little brother's shoulders and Tyson heaved a frustrated sigh, the bitterness coating the back of his throat.

"I have nothing to offer her, absolutely nothing. The ranch house is crap. The business isn't making hardly enough money to keep me afloat. She deserves more and she isn't going to get it from me."

Chance squeezed his shoulders. "What makes you think she wants more? Layla isn't the type of person to go for something if it's not what she wants. Didn't seem to me that she had any trouble slipping into your bed for the weekend when Rory got married."

"That was then, a fling nothing more." He glanced at the house and tried to see it in her eyes, failing miserably to find anything positive about it at all. Up until now it had been perfect. He didn't see the sagging roofline, the peeling paint or the cracked glass in the kitchen windows. He'd been so pleased to be able to buy the rundown ranch, he would have slept in the barn if that was all that was available. To have a rickety old cabin had been the icing on the cake for him. Until now. "Probably a result of too much champagne and the emotions at the time."

"Selling yourself short again." Chance crossed his arms.

"You know her better than I do. Can you honestly see her living in something like this? I mean, it's okay for me because I don't really care, but someone like Layla, not going to happen." He let his shoulders droop, defeat poking him in the back.

"That's your problem. You give up too easily, always did. If you want something, go fight for it. If you only wanted her in your bed for the weekend, why the foul mood now, answer me that one." Chance patted him on the back. "Maybe she's found you a bride."

Tyson whipped his head around, fear knotting in his stomach. "What do you mean?"

"You know that ad you wrote up? I got Layla to deal with it so you didn't get ripped off with someone marrying you only to get their greedy little paws on your ranch when they file for divorce. She's a little harder on people than you would be and I know for a fact there are women out there that marry for profit."

"What the fuck—"

"Hey, don't thank me now. I know you were pissed when I suggested you do it, but it worked for me and Rory so when I saw you'd made a start, I decided to give you a helping hand. Look, I'm not going to let someone rip off my little brother. You might not think this place is worth much to other people but it's what you wanted, what you've worked hard for."

All kinds of horror rumbled around in Tyson's gut. The urge to throw up in the forefront. Chance had given Layla his scribbled advert. How could he? *Holy crap, this is going to be the beginning of the end for me.*

"You bloody idiot! I never said I wanted to go ahead with that. It was whiskey talk, nothing more." He jammed his hands in the back pockets of his jeans to curtail the urge to throw a punch. "That was months ago. I figured you'd forgotten about it. I had."

Chance stood with his hands on his hips and glared at him. "You told me specifically that you would do it. How the hell was I supposed to know you didn't mean it?"

Tyson stamped his feet, the urge to throw a punch at his brother almost too much to hold back. He turned and stormed over to the barn, slammed his fist into the wall and let rip a guttural wail of pain. Wood shattered, the horse bolted down the driveway and splinters of wood pierced his knuckles. "You had no right taking over my life." He turned on his brother, ignored the blood running down his fingers.

"I'd hardly call it taking over." Chance grabbed him by the shoulder, his nails digging into the skin. "You need to calm down and think here."

"What's to think about. You've ruined my life." Tyson pulled away from him and crouched down on the drive, his legs going to jelly. Whatever chance he held of getting Layla to love him had just gone out the window.

"That's bull and you know it. You're being a drama queen again." He gave Tyson a nudge. "Just giving you a heads up because she never said I was to keep her visit a secret. Ball is in your court, brother." He whistled as he walked around his truck to the driver's door, the swagger almost limp free now.

Tyson watched him drive away, his mind wandering to the wedding weekend when Layla had dragged him through the front door of the house and into his bedroom. They'd collapsed onto the unmade bed and that was where they'd stayed for the whole time she was there. Only surfacing long enough for food and a frantic hunt for more condoms. He'd been lucky to find an old box half-filled in the back of the pantry that saw them out for the last day. It had been the best weekend of his life.

And now she was coming back but it wasn't him she'd called. It was Chance. That alone spoke volumes to Tyson.

Chapter Three

"CHANCE HAD TO go and pick up a load of cows so I got to come and collect you. Hope you don't mind?" Callie reached for Layla's bag, slung it over her shoulder as if it weighed nothing and guided her to the front door of the small airport.

"No, that's fine. Good to see you instead, actually. I could to with some girl time, and it's been too long since we had a good chat." Layla was more than pleased Callie was the one waiting for her at the airport. She'd missed the outgoing girl's calm demeanor more than she thought.

"Awesome. So why are you here then, what's wrong?" Callie put her sunglasses on as they walked out into the sunshine.

"Forgot you were a straight shooter." Layla slid her own glasses down from her perfectly smooth hair and perched them on her nose. They walked across the car park to where the truck was parked. Callie threw the bag on the back seat and hopped in the driver's door.

"How's Tyson?"

"Ah, figured it was something to do with him. The way you two were at the wedding and all." The Aussie girl gave Layla a saucy wink reminding her why she liked Callie so much. Nothing much kept her down in the dumps for long and she needed some of that enthusiasm to rub off on her.

"Yes, well, that may be but there's nothing happening there, at least not like you think there is." She smoothed down the pencil thin skirt over her legs and looked out the window at the hive of activity around them wondering if this was going to be enough for her after being in the city for so long.

"Oooh, do tell. Did you want to call into Gina's and have coffee or head straight back to our place?"

"Can we drive through town first, just down the main street? There's a business I want to have a quick look at, then we can go wherever you like." She did up her seat belt as Callie turned on the ignition.

With a quick smile, Callie nodded her head. "Done. This is sounding better and better." She drove out of the airport and headed for the main part of town, and Layla stared out the window.

Denver was the place to be, or so she'd thought all these years. A city girl born and bred, she could think of nothing she liked better than to get involved in the fast track of life. Her job was high-powered and intense most days, just the way she liked it. Changing to move here to a small family law practice would be a huge wake-up call, one she wasn't sure she would handle but this child had to have contact with its father regardless of whether Tyson wanted Layla or not. She wouldn't deny them the opportunity to get to know each other after seeing so many men that never got the chance to know their own offspring and her own sad upbringing.

Being in the business she was, Layla had seen too many broken families and the children were always the ones who came off second best. She wasn't going to let that happen to her child. She would uproot herself, start over in Marietta so her baby could be near its father whether they managed to made a go of their fledgling relationship or not. Not that Layla could say having wild sex for a whole weekend constituted a relationship but there was a spark of something there, had been from the first day she'd met him. Perhaps, if she'd nurtured it enough, it would have blossomed into something they could both live with. *Not going to happen.*

Now she had to try and explain to Tyson how come in this day and age of women who knew their bodies and how to look after them, she'd managed to get pregnant.

Callie slowed as she came to Main Street. "Where exactly did you want to go?"

"Down that way, from memory, near the nail salon they told me." She tried to get her bearings but remembered the last time she was in town.

A business was the last thing on her mind. The heat raced up her cheeks and she turned away to look out the window, hoping Callie wasn't watching her. A sign hung from the storefront balcony and she recognized it from the letterhead on their emails. "There it is. Can you just park out front for a minute? I don't want to go in."

"You're in need of a lawyer? I don't get it, tell me what's going on."

"I put in an offer for it, the business is for sale."

She heard the intake of breath and waited for the questions to come thick and fast. Layla expected nothing less. When silence filled the cab of the truck, she focused instead on the shop front. The white blinds were open and she could see inside. An elderly lady sat at a desk, her hair done up in a bun on top of her head, her glasses pointed at the corners, the type that usually had sparkly fake gems in them. According to the sales rep, Mrs. Emily Forsythe was keen to stay on with the new owner of the business. She had been there for years and was classed as a great asset, too good to let go. Time would tell.

"Sure you don't want to go in and say hello?"

"Perhaps another day." Layla turned and smiled. "Let's go and see Gina and have a coffee. Then I can tell you what I have in mind." She noticed the gleam in Callie's eyes and knew no matter what happened with Tyson, she was among friends.

When they drove into Gina's ranch, Layla leaned forward and smiled as they parked the truck. "It's looking so good. Love what she's done with the front garden, it's so pretty." Years of living in an apartment hadn't given Layla the opportunity to have a garden, not that she had a green thumb or anything but the thought of doing something different was suddenly appealing somehow. *Must be nesting hormones kicking in.*

"She's the perfect, nurturing mother. Great cook, gardener, and baby momma. You should see how big she is now." Callie parked the truck and hurried out, calling as she skipped up the pathway to the door. "Knock knock, honey, we're home."

A squeal and giggle came from the inside of the house seconds before the pounding of tiny feet headed toward the front door. Layla slid from the truck and took a moment to gaze at her surroundings. Calm, peaceful, and very comfortable. Is this what she wanted? Would it be enough to keep her happy after years of playing the high-powered legal brain? Would she be able to cross over into the motherhood game without wanting to slit her wrists in frustration at going from the hectic life she enjoyed to the laid-back family law practice she'd just passed in town? Only time would tell.

"Layla, what are you doing here?"

Before she knew what was happening, she was being wrapped in her friend's arms for an awkward, baby belly in the way kind of hug.

Gina laughed and patted her tummy. "Sorry, things are getting just a little bit awkward already. I'm blowing up like a balloon." She sighed and shared a glance with Callie.

"So come in and tell me what brings you to town, Layla. Not that it's anything but nice to see you but, from the look in your eyes, I'd say this isn't purely a social call." Gina gripped her hand led them inside where Fisher had been playing in his room, intent on his building blocks.

He let go of Callie's hand and reached for Layla. After hugs and kisses he went back to his creations leaving the three women alone in the kitchen.

"Have a seat. Now what can I get you, coffee?"

"Please, that would be great." Layla pulled out a kitchen chair and took a seat at the table, suddenly weary as the rush of adrenaline wore off. She'd made it without balking. Now she had to find the nerve to go and see Tyson. A talk with her friends was what she needed first to bolster her waning energy.

"Hey, are you okay? You've gone very pale." Gina looked at her with concern and Layla knew she was right to come back here.

"Goes with being pregnant I suppose. Although you'd know more about that than I would." She sat back and waited for the fuss.

"I DON'T KNOW what to do, Pa. She's coming back to take care of some business according to Chance and I don't know if she'll want to see me." Tyson sat at his father's kitchen table with a mug of tea gripped between his calloused hands.

"What makes you say that, son?" Jock sipped at his brew and watched his son over the rim of his mug.

"I haven't bothered to call her since the wedding. She's going to think I'm after her for one thing and one thing only if the only time I show an interest is when she's in town." The thought made sense to him.

"Are you?"

"No." He spat out the word. *No, I want more but I doubt I'm what she wants or needs.*

"Well, in that case, I don't understand what's holding you back. If you like her, and I assumed that after what happened at the wedding, you more than liked her, why wouldn't you try and see her. Call at least."

He glanced at his father and looked away, embarrassed, thinking his father knew how he spent the weekend. "And that's not all. I wrote an advert for a wife."

"You did what?" His father screwed up his face and Tyson turned away, not willing to let his father see the shame in his eyes.

He sighed. "I wrote an ad when I was drunk and Chance had someone take care of it for me. I didn't ask him to, he just did it." *Someone.* No way Tyson would let him know how Layla was really involved.

"I DON'T UNDERSTAND. What on earth possessed you to do that after all the crap you gave your brothers for taking that route?"

He shrugged his shoulders. "Who knows. Maybe I'm sick of being alone. Maybe they're not the only ones who need a warm body at night and a woman of their own."

"Yes, but you had Layla."

Tyson snorted.

"What, you think just because these eyes are old they can't see a boy in love? I ain't blind, you know." Jock put his cup down and reached out to pat his son's hand. "Tyson, you know how much I loved your mother, so much you kids suffered for it when she died. Me locking myself away in the bottom of a bottle was wrong and I admit it. At the time I couldn't see past my grief." He coughed to clear his throat and Tyson wondered if he'd ever get over the loss of his wife. "Thing is, her death taught me one thing. If you love someone, make the most of every second. Don't let them get away from you."

"Not that easy, Pa."

"Bull. That wee girl had the hots for you too. I saw the way she looked at you, like she was going to melt if you touched her. That don't mean she wanted a weekend affair to me. I say give her a call or go up to Chance's place and talk to her. You've got nothing to lose and everything to gain."

Tyson looked out the kitchen window, watching the

leaves float from the trees on the soft afternoon breeze. When Chance had come by yesterday and told him Layla was coming to visit he'd wondered why she'd called his brother and not him. Sure, she and Chance had been friends and business acquaintances for years but Tyson was the one who'd slept with her. Surely if she cared, she would have called Tyson instead. But then again why would she? It wasn't as if he'd made the effort to keep in touch with her either. A weekend of mindless sex and he let her go without so much as a "call you later." Not a wonder she'd called Chance instead of him.

"So, why didn't you call her, son?"

"Are you kidding? You've seen her. Big city lawyer. Take a look at me, Pa. I barely make enough to keep the leaky roof I own over my head. Why would she want to tie herself to me when she can have so much more in Denver?" Saying it out loud made it all seem so much more real and sensible.

Why would she want him? His ranch was nothing like his brothers but he still counted himself lucky to have it. If it wasn't for the down payment Chance had given Tyson, he wouldn't even have that. And now with his mail-order bride ad in the papers...

When he first saw the old place he now called home, he'd been hooked. Something about the wide-open space with the mountain backdrop called to him and he was determined to make it his. The fact that the roof leaked and the porch sagged meant nothing to him. It had running water, a decent, old wood stove to cook his food and keep him warm in winter and that was all he cared about. And it had the best set of stables for his horses and a huge barn to keep his winter feed in. What more could a cowboy ask for?

A wife, is what. And only one woman in particular fit the bill. Shame she was too good for him.

"I think you're making a mistake if you let her get away without a fight."

He glanced at his father, wondering if he was right. Pa's pale blue eyes stared back at Tyson from across the table. His lined and tanned face was calmer now than it had been for as far back as Tyson could remember. Making the peace with Chance had been the turning point for their father; it'd given him back his self-respect. Now he could help his eldest son instead of Chance being the family caretaker, taking the brunt of the responsibility as he had done since their mother had died.

"I don't think I have enough to offer her. Simple as that."

Jock shook his head, a sad smile twitching the corners of his lips. "If there's one thing I thought I drummed into you boys it was that you can do and be anything you wanted to."

"That doesn't make it right to punch above your weight. Especially when you know you are."

Jock raised his eyebrow.

"It means go for something better than you are. In this case, Layla is better than me and I think we both know it.

She's a different class to me, everyone can see that. And there's no point in denying I've fucked up again."

Jock stood up from the table and walked around to his son, grabbed him by the shirt, and pulled him from the chair. Tyson went along with it, knowing to fight back would only hurt his father's feelings. And, to be honest, what would be the point?

"Don't you ever let me hear you talking that way again, you hear me?" Jock's face was inches from Tyson's and the pain in his father's eyes made Tyson ashamed of his own feelings. "There is nothing wrong with my sons, nothing at all. You're all good men. This family might not have a lot of money or grown up on the right side of the tracks but nobody can say we aren't hard workers and worthy of respect." He let his hands drop down to his sides. "Now go and sort yourself out. I expect you to bring that lovely little lady around for a cup of tea as soon as you both come to your senses." He walked out of the kitchen leaving Tyson standing by the sink, feeling smaller than he'd ever felt before.

Chapter Four

LAYLA SAT OUTSIDE on the front porch watching Chance saunter up the driveway. He'd offloaded the new cattle into the front paddock and parked the truck when he saw her. When he reached her, he leaned down, kissed her cheek and then perched on the edge of the chair opposite.

"So, tell me what's got you so fired up you had to come out here."

"Looks like some of your wife's traits are rubbing off on you. The Chance I know would have offered me a wine first and spent a few moments making small talk." She wondered how he would take the news.

It was his brother's baby after all, and Chance was more than a little overprotective of all the boys and she understood that. He had played mother and father to them after his own mother died and it was the main reason he'd become a rodeo rider. The money had been too good to turn down and it was also a way to avoid being with his father. Their relationship had been rocky to say the least in the early years.

"Well that was before I really got to know you well and

you became family to me. So, I'll ask again, what's up?"

She let out a sigh. "I'm pregnant."

Chance blinked and stared at her long and hard. "Want me to break his legs for you?"

Layla laughed. "I hardly think that will be a wise decision. It certainly won't fix this problem." She picked at the hem of her blouse, worrying the line of stitches.

"Tyson's or someone else?" His voice had cooled when he said 'someone else.'

"What do you take me for? Of course it's your brother's. I've never been the slutty type and you know it. How many dates have I had lately, huh?"

"I know you two were tight at the wedding..."

"Is that what you call it? I would have said sexed up myself."

"Have you told him?" He eased back in the chair.

"We've not spoken since the wedding. He said something strange to me as I left. Told me 'thanks for taking time out of my fabulous life to give him a weekend he'll never forget.' Like he was shutting the door on me. I don't know, it kind of made me hold back." She knew what he was thinking right now, nothing threw her off. It was why she was such a good lawyer, cutthroat and totally focused. "Kind of like he was saying thanks for the sex and goodbye."

"Why the little..." Chance stood up, his fists clenched.

Layla was immediately on the defensive. "Don't go getting all wound up. It was my own fault, I came onto him so strong and determined to get him into bed and we both know it. Nothing would have stopped me getting him where I wanted him because I'd made up my mind that was that. And I did it, all the chasing, not him. Now I have to decide how to deal with the consequences."

Chance stepped away from her and turned to look over the valley. His back was straight and his shoulders tense. He oozed anger and Layla was sorry she was the reason for it. Would he blame her?

"Look, I only told you because I don't want you to think you have to take my side in this. You don't. You are Tyson's brother and I expect he will need your support more than I will. This is my problem but I want to do the right thing by everyone concerned considering you are all such a close-knit family. I've got every intention of telling Tyson about the baby as soon as I can. And, since he's so intent on finding the right wife and it obviously isn't me, I've also made plans to relocate so he can have access to our child if he wants. I'd never do something so cruel to him as keep the baby away from him."

Chance turned around and looked at her. "You're moving here?"

"Yes. I put an offer in on a family law firm in town. I'm still waiting to see if they accept or not. Then, if they do, I need to start looking for a house to buy and make the move."

"But what if Tyson wants to get together with you and make a go of things? I think it's only fair that you give him that chance, don't you? And this isn't me taking sides either, it seems right is all considering the circumstances."

She smiled, trying not to get emotional over it even though it was hard to ignore the pain. "I can't see that happening. We come from different worlds, Chance. Totally different lifestyles and he never would have made a play for me if I hadn't come onto him so strong." She took a shaky breath and gave him a fleeting smile. "We might be suited in bed but that's the only thing that would work for us. It's not enough." She cupped a hand over her still trim belly. "And the fact he is going to the papers to find a bride and didn't think for one moment to see if I was interested after our time together. Kind of says it all, if you ask me."

It still hurt but she'd have to get over it sooner or later. "You know me though. I'm nothing if not practical. Three months is a long time to not make contact. That to me speaks volumes about how Tyson feels about me. That aside, we can make this work if we put our minds to it. I have support from the girls, so I'll be fine."

"You have mine too, you know that, even though I will always support Tyson, silly young fool that he is. Hell, you and I've been friends for so long now, I'm hardly leaving my business in the city if you're here in town. We go a long way back, Layla. You know I think of you as family. Whatever you need, you can rely on me, both of you can."

If he noticed the tears rolling down her cheeks, he gave no indication.

They were doing the dishes later that night when truck lights came up the driveway.

Callie looked out and winked at her husband. "Here comes trouble."

Layla steeled herself and put down the dishcloth. "If you'll excuse me, I think this is my cue to ruin his little world." She breathed to bring back her calm and headed out to the porch to wait for him.

TYSON SAW HER open the door and step outside as he pulled up and parked. His stomach clenched and his heart pounded in his chest, his nerves getting the better of him. She always managed to put him on tenterhooks. Layla was such a beautiful woman and it scared the hell out of him when she put the moves on and took him to bed. He wasn't used to such forward treatment from a lady, especially one as pretty and high-class as she was.

When he was growing up in the shadow of his older brothers, he was more often the butt of jokes and had a hard time making small talk to the girls. Instead he hid behind a façade, finding it easier to pretend he didn't care or to be someone else.

Layla's white pants clung to her legs and stopped short of her ankles. Ankles he had had his mouth around not that long ago. She had the tiniest little feet, feet that were now bare on the wooden porch A flowing top that gathered under her breasts fell in soft folds leaving her arms bare. The bright splash of colors only made her white blonde hair look paler in the evening light and he itched to run his fingers through the soft strands, pulling her mouth down to his, remembering the tricks that mouth had gotten up to a few short months ago.

He turned off the engine and grabbed his hat from the seat beside him. Time to go and see what was going on.

He opened the door and climbed out. "Layla."

"Tyson." She stood with her hands behind her back watching him walk up to the porch.

He stepped up and stopped before he reached her. "How are you?"

He watched as she licked her lips and tried to smile at him. The smile didn't make it to her eyes and his stomach sunk. He'd done something very wrong.

"We need to talk, Tyson. Did you want to do it here or walk down the lane?"

He glanced inside. Chance and Callie had probably headed for the living room and were already cuddling on the couch. "Here's fine." He took a step over to the corner post and leaned on it, trying for an unaffected pose. "Right, how about you tell me what's going on then?"

"Okay." She moved over and sat down on a chair, her feet together and her hands clasped on her knees. "First off I want to tell you that I don't hold you responsible. I'm an adult and as such I feel it only fair to take half the blame." She licked her lips again before looking up at him. "I'm pregnant, Tyson." Layla took a deep breath and hurried on. "I've already thought about the best way to deal with this. You and I are not compatible apart from in bed, we've proven that already. Neither of us have called each other and you're busy looking for a new wife so because of this and our backgrounds, I've come up with a plan that I hope works for both of us. I've put in an offer for a business in town and will be moving as soon as I can arrange everything. You can have shared custody of the baby when its born."

The air sucked from his lungs with a powerful *whoosh* leaving him light in the head, his ears ringing. *Pregnant? That couldn't be right. Shared custody. Was she serious?* He blinked and tried to focus on her but she was blurry and he couldn't see her properly. He turned from her and stepped off the porch onto the driveway, stumbling to his truck. Tyson leaned on it with both palms held fast on the warm metal of the hood, letting his head drop down between his arms.

Breathe, for goodness sake. Holy shit, this couldn't be happening to him. Not freaking possible!

"Tyson, are you alright?" He felt her hand on his back and flinched. She quickly withdrew from him and he turned to face her.

"You think that because you have more money and education than I do, we can't make this work between us? How could you, how on earth could you…"

She whirled away before he could finish talking but not before he saw the gleam of tears in her eyes. "Go away, Tyson. Just go away." Layla hurried up the porch and into the house, slamming the door behind her.

Good job, pal. That showed her how much you want her. Freaking idiot.

Minutes later Chance came storming out of the house and over to him. He grabbed Tyson by the shirt collar and threw him against the door of his truck, knocking the wind out of him. "Just what the hell do you thing you're doing? I really wanted to support you through this, Tyson, but Layla is in there bawling her eyes out because you blamed her for getting pregnant, you little snot. Last time I checked it took two." His eyes flashed and Tyson was taken back to their childhood when he was the one always on the end of his brother's temper. "You might be my little brother but she is a friend of mine and the mother of your child, whether you want it or not, and you will be respectful of her. Is that understood?"

"I didn't—"

"I said, is that understood?"

Tyson nodded, knowing nothing would make his brother stop until he got his own way. "Yeah."

Chance pulled him up so they were nose to nose. "Don't ever forget it or you'll have me to deal with." He threw him back and Tyson stumbled against the truck. "Might be a good idea for you to leave now. You've done all the damage she can deal with tonight." He turned on his heel and stormed back into the house, slamming the door and locking it, leaving Tyson in no doubt that he wasn't welcome.

He stumbled into his truck and sat holding the steering wheel, his gaze on the darkened porch. Pregnant. Carrying his child. His gut a swirling mix of emotions, threatened to disgrace him but he couldn't focus on driving away. Not while he felt this shaken.

Later that night he lay in his bed, his emotions a jumble of pain alternated with flashes of joy. The woman of his dreams was having his baby. But why on earth was she blaming herself? He was the one who had the old condoms tucked in the back of the pantry. Perhaps if he'd told her just how long they'd been sitting on the shelf they could have found another way to seek pleasure but at the time he couldn't think properly. She did something to him, left him speechless and weak like a newborn foal that couldn't find its feet.

How the hell was he going to make it up to her? And would she want him to anyway? There had to be a way to fix this. Pressing times called for a visit to his brother Rory. Always the peacemaker in the family, he was the one who teased Tyson the least. He was also the one who stood between him and Chance when the need arose and that was usually a fair bit in their younger years. This would be the first time since Tyson brought the ranch that Chance had threatened him physically. He rolled over and punched the pillow, cursing his bad timing and foul choice of words. It wasn't what he was trying to say that hurt her, it was what he managed to get out before his emotions stopped him from finishing the question.

He needed help and he needed it now.

Chapter Five

"YOU SAID WHAT?" Rory looked at him over the beef on rye sandwich in his hand.

Tyson looked around the cafeteria and winced. Two of the police officers glanced their way, the thought of juicy gossip too much to ignore.

"Keep your voice down or I won't tell you."

"Of course you will. Since when have you been able to keep a secret anyway?"

"Not like I was trying to be the town gossip." He glanced at Rory who was looking at him with undisguised disbelief. "I wasn't. You guys wouldn't talk to me unless I had something exciting to tell you. Is it any wonder I made stuff up and then sought out the juicy tittle-tattle? I needed to belong too, you know." As much as he hated to admit to it, he figured it was time to put the record straight. Sick of being called the town gossip, Tyson needed to shake off that label.

Rory frowned and then looked ashamed. "I'm sorry. I didn't know, you should have said."

"Oh, come on. As if you would have believed me anyway. To you guys I was the annoying little brother who was only tolerated when you wanted something." He shrugged his shoulders. "I think it's time I was treated the same as you treat the others."

"Fair enough I suppose. Now tell me what's got you all in a lather. Gina said she had a visitor yesterday but won't say anything because it's not her business."

"Layla's in town. She's staying at Chance's place."

"Oh, I see. And she has you all hot and bothered under the collar just like at the wedding, eh?" He grinned and punched Tyson on the shoulder.

"Kind of. She's pregnant."

Rory's jaw dropped and he was lost for words, something that never happened before.

"And I said the wrong thing." He rubbed his hand over his chin, watching the change in his brother's eyes. "I know, I know, if my mouth was any bigger I'd get both feet in it." He sighed.

"What happened? Tell me from the top and don't leave anything out if you want my help." Rory watched the two officers leave the lunchroom and gazed back at Tyson.

Just thinking about this was painful. "You know we left together at your wedding. I think everyone saw that." He grimaced. "Anyway, we had a great time. She's all I could ask for and more but I didn't think things would go beyond great sex over the weekend. I mean, look at her and look at me."

Rory put his sandwich down, folded his arms and looked, saying nothing and for that Tyson was grateful.

"Anyway, I didn't call her, thinking if she wanted more she would call me. I didn't want to pressure her, you know, the country hick hitting on the slick, city lawyer." He copped a kick to the ankle when he said that. Tyson frowned but didn't lean down to rub the aching bone deciding it would only get him another kick. "I have nothing to offer her. Don't care what Pa says, my place is rundown and I can barely afford to feed me let alone a wife. What woman would want to move into something like my little rundown house? It's nothing like what you have."

"Have you forgotten what Gina found when she arrived at my place?"

"Yeah but at least you had the money to fix it. I don't, not yet anyway."

Rory watched him, arms crossed.

"So anyway, the other day Chance pops over and tells me she's coming to visit only she visits him not me. And that he let her place an ad for a wife for me."

"He what?" Rory sat forward, his mouth open.

"I got drunk after she left, alright? Tried to drown my sorrows and Chance convinced me to write an ad." He glanced at Rory, suddenly defensive. "Look, it worked for you, why shouldn't I have a turn?"

Rory leaned further across the table into his face. "But, as I recall, brother, you were royally pissed at us for doing it.

And why on God's earth would you even contemplate that when you have the likes of Layla drooling over you?"

"Why do you think?" Rory continued to stare. "I have nothing to offer her. Why would I even try?"

"You're an idiot, you know that, right?"

"At least hear me out. I was never going to put that in the paper. It was Chance's fault. Nosy bastard took it from my house and gave it to Layla to deal with. I knew nothing about it until he told me she was coming to stay."

"I don't believe you, Tyson."

He bristled. "It's the truth. You can ask Chance."

Rory rolled his eyes. "Continue."

"Last night, I went over to see her and she tells me she's pregnant and next thing I know Chance has me pushed against my truck threatening me with all sorts of bodily harm."

"Sure. It's never that simple, Tyson. From what I hear, you gave her a mouthful."

"I did not. I couldn't get the damned words out is what happened. She only heard half of what I was trying to say and freaked out." He hung his head. "Then Chance wouldn't let me say anymore. Sent me packing." He glanced at Rory. "Thought you didn't know anything."

"Chance called me. What were you trying to say then?"

"That how could she not hold me responsible. I was the one who supplied the condoms." He blushed under his brothers unwavering scrutiny. "I only got out half that sentence."

"How could she… you mean that part?" Rory shook his head as if he knew the answer.

"Yeah." Shame crept up his neck.

"You idiot. Can you imagine how that must sound to a woman who is baring her soul to you? Announcing that she is going to have a baby, your baby?"

"I know, I understand that." Frustration made Tyson cranky and he knew better than to try and take it out on his brother. Rory was the only one who would help him out. "I want to go and see her but I'm afraid to put my foot in it again."

"You don't have any choice the way I see it. Go grovel and get it over and done with, the sooner the better. I'd also tell her that you only wrote that ad in a fit of despair or something similar. See if you can salvage a relationship with her. Either way, whether you two make a go of it or not, you have a child to think of. That's bigger than you or her and your desires. At least prove to me you can act like a man and take responsibility for your mistakes. And if you used a condom, how on earth did you get her pregnant?"

"Um, I think, I mean, they were kind of old." He ducked the palm doing its best to connect with the side of his head.

TYSON WAS OUT when Layla decided to go down to visit. She'd cried herself to sleep over his comments last night but today in the dull light of early morning, she thought it over and decided to give him another chance. Of course he was stunned. So was she when she found out she was carrying his child. Stunned, excited, and terrified all at the same time. It was enough to make anyone lost for words or incapable of a decent conversation. He deserved more and she was prepared to give him the benefit of the doubt as she remembered her own feelings. And she knew how words or lack thereof could affect the outcome of a particularly bad situation. Heaven knew she'd seen it often enough in the course of her day job. One more chance to talk things through without emotions getting in the way. At least that was the idea when she arrived.

Finding no one at home when she got there had thrown that plan into the wind.

Teary now and annoyed with herself for feeling that way, Layla stood on the sagging porch and looked around. There was a certain amount of charm in the ramshackle old ranch house. She'd imagined Rory and Gina's place was very similar when they brought it listening to conversations and it had turned out fine once the renovation was finished.

Tyson didn't have that kind of money but Layla certainly did. Not that he would accept it and not that she would offer if she was living in town but if their child was going to be spending any amount of time here on the ranch, the least she could do was contribute to some of its upkeep. Make it safe.

She tried the door and found it unlocked. That weekend they'd spent in bed was the only time she felt alive outside of the courtroom and she ached for a reminder if only for a moment. Her life was one big round of appointments, meetings, and the law. Hardly any time in the last eight years since she'd finished studying had been for her or her enjoyment alone. That was why, when she laid eyes on Tyson standing outside at Chance's place, she'd let her attention wander and focused on him.

And boy had she noticed him. Her hormones had stood to attention and literally sang with joy when he looked her way, his eyes showing how interested he was.

He was younger than her, but only by a year or two and she was smitten enough to not care about marks on a calendar. After all, it was only a number. Tyson was a good-looking man. Ruggedly handsome, not uncouth exactly, but more like a person who was cozy in their own skin without the glam and shine she was used to. Shut off from the big, outside world, untouched almost. And that appealed to her because she was feeling particularly jaded with her life. Someone as unassuming as Tyson made her feel like a different person, a person she yearned to be, if only for the weekend.

When she finished up the case for Rory and Gina, she'd jumped at the chance to come back for their wedding. It meant she got to spend more time with the family she'd bonded with and the handsome cowboy who'd piqued her curiosity and her libido. In him, she saw herself before the law made her immune to the nastiness of people. Tyson thought good of most and it was refreshing. And she soon found out he was incredible in bed. So good that she didn't want to leave and go back to Denver but theirs was a relationship that wouldn't last and she had responsibilities.

She had them now but they were changing. There was a baby to think of and he or she would come first from now on.

Layla stepped into the small, rustic kitchen, directly off the porch. Tyson's breakfast dishes sat on the draining board on the small kitchen counter. A red and white check tea towel hung over the door of the woodstove, a basket of chopped wood sat tucked in the corner of the room ready for use. She wandered through an open door into the family room. His big armchair sat in front of the television set, the only modern appliance in the house. An old coffee table next to it covered in horse magazines and newspapers.

The gold and brown carpet had seen better days and came right out of the seventies but that didn't bother her. Tyson's bedroom door stood open and she felt drawn to it just as she had a mere few months ago. He hadn't made the bed back then either. The sheets were rumpled as if he'd had a bad night. A pillow lay crumpled and ignored on the floor and she leaned down to pick it up, bringing it to her nose. The smell of him made her eyes water. *Damned hormones.*

Nobody warned her about them, the constant tears and the mood swings.

"Oh, Tyson, where did this go so wrong?" She hugged the pillow to her chest and sank to the bed, sobbing uncontrollably as the floodgates she'd held closed finally opened.

Eventually she lay down with the pillow clutched against her breast, not willing to let go of the only contact she had. Last night hadn't gone as planned and, as much as she'd promised herself she would be cool and professional over this, seeing him had ruined everything.

A car door slammed and she startled. Should she walk out casually pretending nothing was wrong?

His voice called out. "Chance, you in there?" *Of course, I have the truck and he thinks it's his brother.*

Layla kicked her feet down and tried to stand up but a wash of dizziness came over her and she moaned, falling back onto the bed.

"Layla?" The door slammed and footsteps sounded her way.

Tyson hurried in and stood at the bedroom door. She tried to speak but couldn't find the words, tears blocked her throat. He stepped over and knelt in front of her and took her hands in his. The rough skin grazed against her soft palms.

"Are you okay? You've gone as white as a sheet." He brushed her hair from her forehead and eased her back on the bed until her head hit the pillow. Then he moved to lift her feet up so she could stretch out. "Shhh, rest a minute. It's okay." He held her hand in one large fist and with his free hand, stroked her hair.

Her tears ran freely down her cheeks, pooling in the slant of her nose before rolling over and down her other cheek and soaking his pillow. Layla sniffled and took a couple of steadying breaths. This wasn't how she wanted it to be.

Chapter Six

TYSON SAT ON the edge of the bed holding Layla's hand and watched the color slowly come back into her face. His gut ached, watching her cry, but he wasn't sure he had the right words to make her feel better. As much as she made his body stand up and take attention, he still wasn't convinced he could offer her a decent life. In his mind, this baby would probably bring them together but surely the passion would eventually wane and things would go downhill from there, just as she had said. He could see it in his mind. That was no life for a child, especially his.

She shuffled over and inched her way up the bed to a sitting position, his pillow still gripped against her chest.

"Feeling better?"

Layla nodded her head.

"Listen, about last night. What I was trying to say didn't come out right." She met his gaze and then looked away. "What I was trying to say was, how could you blame yourself when it was all my fault." Tyson looked at the ground, focusing on the tip of his boots, the leather scuffed and almost worn through at the point.

He needed new footwear but there were other things that he needed more. New saddles, blankets, and bridles, if he was going to open the ranch up for trail riding, and fencing and the list went on and on.

She spoke, her voice trembling. "I'm pretty sure I had something to do with it. You might as well know that the first time I met you I promised myself I'd get you into bed and I got my wish." She shrugged her shoulders. "Not saying I'm proud of myself but what's done is done. No point in blaming each other or ourselves for that matter. I'm strong enough to know we can get through this if we put our minds to it."

She already had a plan and she hadn't consulted me before making up her mind. I was right all along. I'm not good enough for her no matter what Pa and Rory say. Not that what Chance did helped my cause in any way.

He would play this close to his chest for now. "Care to share again what that might be? I was in shock and didn't really take it in last night."

She looked at him with cool blue eyes and he could see the moment she went into lawyer mode, leaving the crying woman of seconds ago, behind. Layla ceased to be the lover who was warm and pliable under him, she became the focused domineering woman he first met at Chance's. Tough and intent on winning. There would be no changing her mind, this he knew.

"I'm moving to Marietta. I've put an offer in on a family

law firm in town and I'll find a suitable place to live. I want our child to have access to both parents, Tyson, as well as your brothers and their children. You might not believe me but there's nothing I want or need from you. I don't want there to be any animosity between us and I know firsthand that you've moved on with your life."

"About that, I didn't…

She held up her hand. "Stop right there. I don't need, nor do I want to know about the whys and wherefores of this process we have going to find you a bride. It is what it is and I'll do what I promised Chance. We don't need to discuss it."

She cleared her throat and glanced at him from under her lashes. "I've seen far too many relationships torn apart that damaged children in my career to wish that on my own child. My own upbringing left much to be desired."

Tyson went to put his arm around her but she held up her hand.

She took another deep breath. "My parents loved me, I know they did but they both had their high-powered careers to think about, which meant I saw more of the housekeeper than I saw of them and I refuse to let my child grow up that way. He or she needs to come first and that is why I've turned my back on my career to move here and make sure you can be involved. Part-time parenting doesn't cut it with me. I plan to share raising this baby with you and I'd appreciate it if you wouldn't fight me on this. After careful consideration, I think it's best for all concerned."

"Is there any point me trying to have my say, Layla? How can you make up your mind already without giving me a chance?" She had, he could see it plain as day.

He had been right all along, he wasn't worthy enough to be with her. Tyson supposed he should be glad she at least told him about the child and her plans to share its upbringing with him but he didn't feel as though he was winning. He felt used and abused, given the short straw in this scenario. She'd had time to think all of this through and he'd only had a day, and not really even that.

He had to fight for what he wanted. "I thought there was something between us, something we could work with."

Layla shuffled around, put her feet on the ground and stood up, glancing down at him. "It was fun and you're a great guy and all but the thing is, I don't need you, Tyson." She looked out the window. "Besides, you'd already decided to move on before I found out I was pregnant, so let's leave things how they are. I've thought long and hard about this. I want what's best for this baby and having two parents who can help raise it without wanting to kill each other is the best way."

"Even if those two parents aren't together?" Now it made sense why she'd never called after the wedding.

He was an urge, an impulse, and nothing more. A roll in the hay for the high-flying city lawyer, nothing more. Distaste rose in his throat. Who'd of thought Tyson would ever have reason to think of himself as a man whore? It didn't go down well.

"There has to be a way for us to fix this, Layla. I don't think it's fair that you make the rules without giving me a chance. Can we go back to how it was at the wedding? Surely we haven't changed that much in, what – three months?"

"You have, as far as I'm concerned."

"What's that supposed to mean?" Tyson demanded.

"Tyson, you wanted a mail-order bride," Layla said cool-ly.

"That was Chance's doing," Tyson denied sick of this topic because he felt like she'd already judged him guilty. "I don't want a mail-order bride for goodness sake. I want you."

Layla turned so he couldn't see her face and for a brief moment he had a sliver of hope. Her shoulders rose with each breath and he counted one, two, three before she turned back to him.

She smiled, albeit sadly and shook her head. "It won't work between us. We're too different and I think deep down you know this. The last thing I want to do is break your heart, Tyson, but I'd rather do it now than later. You know what they say about taking off a plaster quick to cause less pain? I thought about it a lot and that's the decision I've come to. Regardless of what either of us might want, I think this is for the best."

SHE STUMBLED OUT of the bedroom, willing him to stop her and beg her to stay but he didn't. Playing tough to protect her already fragile heart was hard but Layla figured it was going to be easier in the long run. Having him profess a love he didn't feel for her now, and watching as that emotion drained day after day as they tried to make a go of the situation they'd found themselves in wasn't a path she wanted to take.

Not again. One relationship that didn't work for almost the same reasons was enough for her in this lifetime. She'd considered Samar to be the love of her life. Their final year of law school had thrown them together. Their different cultures didn't matter to the two young lovers, nor did the fact his family were of importance in their hometown. Her family was wealthy if not as important as Samar's. Besides Layla and Samar were very much in love and they brushed off the negatives of their relationship. Until he'd wanted to marry her and told his family of his plans to propose.

Layla had been gutted when he left, citing their differences in ways that he'd professed hadn't mattered before. Now they had broken her heart. She made a solemn promise to herself to be the person making the decisions for her future.

Until she'd met Tyson. He triggered something in her that she couldn't explain. A gentleness that reminded her of who she used to be before she hardened her heart to the world. But the old nagging of her earlier decision overrode the desire he sparked in her once she'd flown home.

Far better to do this now than down the track when she'd become used to having Tyson around. Before she became used to loving him and his touch on her skin, the sensations he caused to ripple over her body and make her feel alive.

She paused, her hand on the door of the truck and took a final look around. She had almost convinced herself she could have been happy here, if there was love between them, but that didn't seem to be the case. Together they could have worked to make the ranch profitable. She'd lain against his chest and listened to his voice as he'd described what he wanted to do when he had the money. Horses were his love and the wilderness in which he looked so much the part it made her heart ache. This cowboy would never fit into her way of life, not here nor in the city. He was too rugged and in touch with the land he lived on to want to be with her.

The only Watson boy not to leave town when he was old enough, Tyson had stayed close to his father and learned the hard way how to look after himself. He could take off into the mountains for a week and come out the other side happy and refreshed, whereas, if she took him to the city, he would wilt and fade. She couldn't do that to him, change him to suit her lifestyle. And she didn't know if she had it in her to change as much as he would need her to so she fitted in.

Layla had chosen her future well, or so she told herself. This child would want for nothing. Surrounded by an extended family, it would grow up with the best of both worlds, its father's outdoor life and her more genteel, privileged upbringing.

She opened the truck door and slid behind the wheel, glancing at the house to see if she could get one more glimpse of the man she loved but couldn't have. The drive up the hill to Chance and Callie's almost broke her heart all over again. It felt as though she was saying goodbye to what might have been. A silly notion Layla put down to pregnancy hormones.

Callie stood on the porch with a mug of coffee in her hand when Layla drove up. Her cattle dog, Sherbet, hurried over and sniffed around Layla's feet.

"Sherbet, that's enough." Callie watched her. Layla would have to talk about what happened.

It was part of the deal being friends with the Watson women, something Layla didn't really mind. It was comforting to have the shoulder to cry on and the advice that followed.

"You're not looking too good. Need a coffee or a good cry? I have a spare shoulder right now."

"I think I'm going to need both." Her eyes misted with tears as she stepped up onto the porch.

Callie put down her mug and opened her arms, wrapping them around Layla, hugging tight as she leaned on her friend and let the tears flow. It was all she could do to hold onto Callie and not rush down the hill to Tyson and tell him she was sorry, she'd made a mistake, and they needed to bring up this child together.

The hand rubbing her back slowed and Callie shifted. "You okay now?" She peered into Layla's eyes and the concern on her face was the thing that made Layla hold her ground.

She had all the support here if she needed it and she was sure whatever decisions she made in the future, Callie would have her back.

"Yeah, thanks." She took a tissue from her pocket and dabbed at her eyes before giving her nose a good blow. It felt better to get the tears out of her system so she could focus on the future and the things she had to do right now. "I really needed that."

"Are you sure you're doing the right thing here? I mean, what if Tyson wants to be with you and raise this baby, don't you think he deserves that chance?"

Layla picked up her now cold coffee and tasted it, grimacing before tossing the distasteful liquid onto the grass. Once her favorite drink, an aversion to the taste was growing.

"I've thought it through. It's all I did when I found out. We're too different to make this work, Callie. It sounds like I'm being a snob but I don't mean to be. I've been burned before. We want different things and have different goals.

Tyson's are firmly set and I get that." She looked down in the direction of his ranch. "It might have worked for a while and that would be great but I don't think I could go through the heartache down the road when the passion fades. Not with a child between us, that's so unfair."

"Didn't he even try to stop you?"

Pain shot through her heart and she winced. "No."

"I'm sorry, honey. I know how much you're hurting."

"I'm not the first woman to find herself pregnant and alone. Certainly won't be the last." She took a deep breath of the cool mountain air, taking the time to settle her wildly beating heart. She could still do this. Layla was nothing if not dedicated and once she made up her mind, she followed through. "Guess I'd better find out what's happening with the offer I made on the business. I have a life to get sorted out before this little one makes an appearance."

Chapter Seven

IT TOOK TWO months for Layla to settle on the business and sell her apartment in Denver, pack up her life and make the move to Marietta. In that time, she had several responses to Tyson's advert. Only two she deemed feasible and passed them on to Tyson via Chance and heard no more about them.

Callie, Chance, and Gina kept in touch with her regularly and she felt as though she was moving home when she drove up the main street one sunny afternoon. She headed straight to her new office and parked out front. The name had been changed on the glass window and the overhead hanger and it made her smile to see 'Cox Family Law Firm' there. Gave her a sense of place she badly needed.

She climbed out of her car and stood rubbing her back. The drive had been long and she'd broken it up by staying in a motel along the way. Now five and a half months pregnant, she got tired easily and it was uncomfortable with such a long time spent in the car. Chance had suggested she ship her vehicle and fly but Layla had wanted the time to get her head together. The drive was her way of doing that.

She pushed the door open and walked in. Her secretary, Emily Forsythe was on the telephone, busily writing notes as she spoke.

"Yes, that's right. Ms. Cox is taking appointments starting tomorrow. Yep, she sure is sharp, you mark my works. Just moved here from Denver." She paused for breath. "Ten o'clock? Righto then, Rupert. We'll see you then. Bye now." She hung up the phone and made a note in her calendar before looking up.

"Well, well. You're a sight for sore eyes." She bustled around the desk and took a bemused Layla by the arm. "Look worn out, you do. Come and have a seat and I'll get you a cup of tea." Once Layla was sitting down, Emily patted Layla's arm and smiled. "You need to take care of yourself little lady. I'm not going to let you overdo things around here either. Promised Chance I'd keep an eye on you and I will. Now relax while I put the kettle on." She hurried off to the little kitchenette and Layla could hear her fussing around with cups and a tray. A few moments passed before she came back out, carrying a tray with cups and a plate of homemade biscuits.

"It's good to see you, Ms. Cox. Been keeping an eye out all day for you. Bet you're glad you finally made it. You must be exhausted with that big drive."

"Call me Layla, please. It was a long drive and I'm rather tired but very pleased to be here finally. Feels as though this has taken forever to sort out." She took the china cup and sipped the hot tea, letting it slide pleasantly down her throat. "Oh, that is perfect. I needed this."

"My cure-all for just about everything." Emily pushed her glasses up her nose and smiled. "Got you a few appointments already. As you heard when you came in, one of our locals, Rupert Hanson is coming in tomorrow to sort out his will. Those grandsons of his are causing him no end of trouble. Nothing a good whipping and some hard work wouldn't sort out, if you ask me." She shook her head. "You'll probably get to know them sooner or later. They're always in trouble, and you'll probably get called upon to haul them out of jail more often than you'd like. Seems they end up in there regular as clockwork much to Rory's annoyance."

"Sounds like fun times." She leaned her head back against the wall and looked around the waiting room. It was peaceful, sitting in here amongst the pale green decor and the potted plants. A box of children's toys sat in a corner beside a tiny table and chairs with scrap paper for drawing to keep them entertained. Comfy chairs and a coffee table were positioned on the other side of the waiting room which was where she sat now, recovering from her long drive.

"The movers finished yesterday and Gina and Callie brought the keys back this afternoon after they finished fussing around, 'sorting out the basics' they said so you could at least sleep in your own bed tonight. They said to call if you needed anything."

"They're very kind." All she wanted to do was crawl into bed and close her eyes.

"And Gina made you a meal or two from what I can gather. She said look in the fridge when you get there." Emily smiled over her glasses. "Your telephone is on as well and I've arranged for a man to mow your lawns. Jock put his hand up and wouldn't take no for an answer."

"Jock Watson?" That felt weird. The grandfather of her unborn child mowing her lawns.

"Yes. I wasn't sure how you would feel about that and since I don't really know you that well, figured it wasn't my place to get uppity over it."

"That's fine. I'll speak to him. Thank you." Layla finished her tea and placed the cup on the tray, helping herself to a biscuit. She crunched it hungrily, wondering how long ago it was she ate. "These are good, Mrs. Forsythe." She took another one and sat back eating contentedly.

"That's enough of the Mrs. Name's Emily and, since you and I are going to be working together, it's only right you call me that. Now let me get you another cup of tea, looks like you need to replenish the batteries." Emily hurried to the kitchen and came back with a fresh cup, placing it in front of Layla.

"I can't believe how hungry and thirsty I am." Layla rubbed her hand over the growing baby bump.

"From what I remember, pregnancy does that to you. Now don't go overdoing things around here or you'll get me shot. I made a promise I'd take care of you in the office and I will unless you say otherwise."

"I appreciate the concern, really I do. And these cookies, if you keep feeding me these, I'm going to have problems later on losing the weight."

"I hardly think so. You're as thin as anything apart from the baby bump."

Layla spent a relaxing half hour drinking tea and nibbling on biscuits before she decided it was time to head for her new home. The small cottage close-by had been leased for twelve months and she was keen to see how it looked with her own furniture inside. She stood up and gathered her car keys.

"Tomorrow I'll be in around eight. Thanks for looking after things for me, Emily, very much appreciated."

"It's what I'm here for. Sleep well and I'll see you bright and early in the morning."

As Layla drove toward her cottage, she wondered if Tyson was dealing with this any better than she was. Many a night since she'd made her decision, she'd rolled over, imagining he was there, his face taunting her in her dream state. Not once since he'd found out about the baby had he tried to contact her to convince her to change her mind. That hurt more than anything. He was probably busy wooing his new bride to be.

Callie hadn't said much about him either no doubt being careful not to mention his name and business so as not to upset the expectant mother. He was keeping to himself, working hard with his broncos and setting up trail rides was all she'd heard. Sounded like he'd moved on.

JOCK DROVE UP and parked near the barn and Tyson sighed. If this was another lecture, he didn't need it. His father got out of his station wagon and walked to the back, lifting up the back door. He reached in and pulled out a western saddle, old but sturdy.

"What's that for?" Tyson met him across the driveway and took it from his father's arms. He walked over to the barn and threw it over the post and rail fence.

"What do you think it's for? There's another two in in the car for you." Jock turned and walked back dragging out another one. He handed it to his son and reached for the last one. A bag of bridles lay on the front seat of the car and he reached in for them as well. Once he offloaded the saddle, he pulled out bridles, laying them over the fence so Tyson could see what he'd brought.

"Thought you could use them since you want to get your trail riding up and going. Can't go far with what you've got."

Tyson picked up a bridle and ran his hands over it. *Old but in good condition.* "Where did these come from?"

"Don't really matter. He was selling them cheap and you needed them." His father nodded his head as if it was that simple.

"How much did you pay?" He was going to have to find the money somewhere to pay him back.

"Not telling. Don't go looking a gift horse in the mouth, son. My contribution to you."

"Pa, you don't have to do this. I'll manage somehow." His plans for the ranch would all come together eventually.

Raising his bucking broncos had started to pay off. They were selling well to the rodeo circuit and he had kept the best mares for breeding. After selling on the already broken in horses to Rory earlier in the year, Tyson had stopped to think. If he branched out and kept the calmest of the horses, he could hire them out as trail riders.

Every auction he went to pick up broncos seemed to have sturdy horses ready for the glue factory that nobody wanted, going for a song. It was a crying shame because there was nothing wrong with them, they'd just lost their usefulness to their current owner or had a bit of age on them. With a little love and feed, they would turn out to be reliable horses and it wasn't as though he didn't have the room to set up trails.

The idea to have a trail ranch had come slowly but surely into being. His love of horses was well known and his animals were always looked after. He had the space and the time to make sure the trails were clear and his ranch had the scenery that pulled in riders like bees to honey.

There was nobody who knew the mountains like Tyson

did. During the years of family breakdown and discord, his go to place had always been the mountains. Trekking and hiking with his school group, his friends, and anyone he could latch on to, had been what kept him sane. It hadn't taken long for it to be what drove him, pushed him to know more. His love of the outdoors had given him a sense of purpose, a goal to learn as much as he could with the dream that one day he would own his own piece of Copper Mountain.

It made sense to broaden that side of the business. The only thing holding him back had been the lack of money. But slowly it was all coming together and having his family pick up the odd bargains like Pa today made it all so much easier.

"Thanks, Pa. You did good." He patted his father on the back.

"Layla arrived in town the other day. Moved into the little cottage around the road from me."

"Uh-huh."

"So, aren't you going to go over and see how she is? Getting quite a decent belly on her from all accounts."

"She made it perfectly clear what she thinks of me. You know that so stop pushing it." He picked up a saddle and walked into the tack room with it, dumping it on one of the empty racks. *When was his father going to give up? Layla didn't want him.*

"Seems to be making a name for herself in town already.

Rupert reckons she has a mind like a steel trap. Went in and changed his will so those no good grandsons of his don't squander the ranch when he dies."

"Good for him."

"Don't think the boys took it too well either. But you know them, hotheads the lot of them. Not like my boys." He shook his head. "No sir, never had no reason to worry about you boys turning out right. Not even with me being the worst father out there."

Tyson shook his head and gazed at the man who'd raised him. "Pa, you weren't the worst father. You had issues but I knew you still loved us." It had been hard growing up but they'd all survived and now his father was on the wagon, things had gotten better for all of them.

"Thing is, Tyson, I don't want you to go down the same path. Regardless of how you two feel about each other, you need to get on for this baby. Don't be hiding out here on the ranch like having a family don't mean nothing to you."

"I'm not—"

His father cut him off with the raise of a hand. "Yes, you are and don't argue with me. You know I'm right. You haven't been to any family dinners at Chance's, Evan's, or Rory's. You've hardly been into town lately. It's like you've avoided all of us since Layla announced she was pregnant. We notice these things, son. Hell, it was your idea to catch up as a family once a week for a meal and since Layla made her announcement you're the one missing. Don't seem right somehow to hide yourself away from the family when you need us." His father reached out and gripped his arm. "Come to dinner tomorrow. For me."

"I have enough to do here. Got some bookings for this weekend and I want to make sure things are just right." He looked away, embarrassed his father would see through his lies.

He had been avoiding them all. Chance was good friends with Layla and she had the support of his brother and his wife, so feeling at ease at the house was no longer possible. Gina too was very friendly with Layla. Rory was the only one Tyson felt comfortable with these days and he had his own life to deal with twins on the way.

Tyson's problem was his own and that was the way he wanted to keep it. Once the baby was born, he would make contact and sort out shared parenting rights. Until then he was giving her a wide berth. It was too painful to see the way she looked at him and wonder what was going through her mind.

"Come to dinner, son. For me, please." The pain in his father's eyes was the undoing of him.

"Fine."

"Great. Well, I'd better get up the hill to Chance's place. Got to help him bring in some cows for branding this morning." He patted Tyson on the back. "I'll see you up there tomorrow night then for dinner." Tyson watched him walk back to his car and waved as he reversed and drove away.

Chapter Eight

LAYLA CONCENTRATED ON the words in front of her, going over a client's file when there was a knock on her door and it opened. "You have a prenatal appointment up at the hospital."

Layla looked from Emily to the clock on the wall. "I forgot. Thanks for reminding me." She grabbed her car keys and purse and pushed herself out of her chair, pausing to rub her belly.

"Junior been a bit active has he?" Emily smiled. She was fast becoming Layla's surrogate mother and all-round protector.

"Yes, he is. I swear I got no sleep last night. Soon as I lay down he started kicking me under the ribs. He was still rolling around at two a.m."

"In my day, we'd have said that meant you were in for a wild ride in early childhood. Nowadays, I reckon it's pretty normal."

"Yes, I suppose it is. Right, I'll be back soon. Thanks, Emily." She hurried out the door and slipped into her car.

On the short drive to the hospital, Layla pondered over her life in town since she'd moved here. The sense of belonging was wonderful and she'd made more friends here in the short time since the move than she ever did in Denver. But that was to be expected. Her job was a lot less high profile now with a different cliental. Mainly wills and powers of attorney and home sales, something that she used to pass down to another colleague. The odd court case for minor infringements kept her mind active but it was nothing like she was used to and she was finding more and more that the quieter side of business suited her. Who would have thought, the "killer in the courtroom lawyer" would turn into a small, country town fan?

She turned into the hospital parking lot, pulled over into the first free spot she found, and made her way into the hospital and the doctor's rooms. Layla gave her name to the receptionist and sat down with a magazine to wait for her turn.

"Ms. Cox, you can go in now." A smiling nurse held the door open and Layla rose, walked in. Evan waited for her and he held out his hand. "You're looking good." He kissed her cheek and perched on the edge of his desk. "How are you feeling?"

"Tired."

"That's to be expected at this stage. Have you given thought to what I suggested last visit?"

"Cutting back my days? Yes, I have. Only Monday to

Thursday now and I finish midafternoon so I can have a nap."

"Great. I wish all my patients were as easy to deal with as you. Having three Watson woman pregnant at the same time is dicey to say the least. I might have to get you to talk to my wife." He reached for her arm and wrapped the blood pressure cuff around it.

She blushed. "I'm not a Watson woman, Evan, but I get your point. How's Denver doing? I haven't seen her for awhile."

"I'm sorry. I know you and Tyson aren't married but I can't help but think of you as one of the family."

"It's okay, I understand." She watched the gauge rise and fall slowly as he checked her vitals.

"That looks good, a little high but within the boundaries. Denver is being Denver. Fights me every step of the way with this bed resting. She's up in her office if you have time to go and say hello. I've given her two hours then she's to go home and put her feet up."

"You're a lovely husband, Evan. She's a very lucky woman." He helped her up and held her arm as she stepped up to hop on the bed. When she was lying down, he called the nurse in and proceeded to prod her stomach.

"Baby is growing well by the feel of things. I want you to have an ultrasound today. About time we double-checked this little guy's important data."

"Fine. I'll do that straight away and then go up and say

hello to Denver. If I don't get back to work, Emily will worry herself silly."

"You fell on your feet getting her for your secretary. From what I understand, she's taking her mothering duties very seriously." He grinned down at her, wrote a note on her file.

"She's amazing. I was hesitant at first because I thought she'd like to retire but not a chance. The woman is fantastic. Makes sure I look after myself too and she has way more energy than I do, don't know how she does it." Layla sat up with his help and swung her feet over the edge of the bed. "I'll understand if you don't want to discuss this, but how is Tyson?"

Evan looked up and frowned at her. "I thought you two were talking." He tapped his pen on his lip.

"That was the plan but he hasn't contacted me and I haven't called him either. I guessed he was waiting for the baby to be born before he sorted out his fatherly duties."

"So he hasn't even seen a picture of the baby then?"

"No."

"Does he know he's having a boy?"

"I haven't told him." She could feel the heat rising in her cheeks. "How can I, when we don't talk? He doesn't put in an appearance at family gatherings so I figured he was giving me a wide berth."

He shook his head. "You two need a good shaking, honestly you do. Layla, let me be honest here okay? As your doctor and as a friend. I think you're both making a huge mistake."

"I'll take what you say on board, Evan, but it takes two as you know. Now I'd better go and have that ultrasound and catch up with Denver before she goes home."

"I'm sorry you feel this way, but I have to say what I think. You two can butt heads all you like but you're having a baby together and that is something special."

Layla paused and then looked at him, deciding the risk was worth the pain she might get in return. "Has he decided on a bride, do you know?"

"I don't know what you mean."

She raised an eyebrow. "Seriously?"

"Seriously. I thought you two would be getting married and I'm waiting for you to share the news with me. Do I have it all wrong?"

"Yes, you do. Tyson advertised for a wife and I was the one who vetted the replies. I sent two resumes to him a couple of months ago of suitable brides which makes me think he never took the ad down when I told him my news."

"You're kidding me, right?" He wiped a hand over his face and stared at her, face pale with shock.

Layla shook her head and pushed back the emotions. "No. I didn't mean to be the one to tell you but I figured you'd understand my position a little better if you did."

"You could have floored me with that information. Does Rory know?"

Layla shrugged her shoulders. "I think Tyson told him. Gina and Callie know so I guess so."

"Nice of them to pass it along. Layla, I'm really sorry. It should be you he's marrying."

"I don't think so. We're not that suitable, Evan. Too different to make it work. I'd better get a move on if I want to catch up with Denver."

"You take care and tell my wife I'll be up later to take her home."

"Thanks, Evan." She smiled and walked out without saying another word about Tyson.

Disappointment burned as she left the doctor's clinic. She still wanted Tyson more than she thought possible. Lying alone in bed at night holding on to her stomach while their baby kicked and moved was gut wrenching and more often than not she cried herself to sleep. It wasn't only the baby's nocturnal movements that kept her awake. The longer this pregnancy progressed, the harder it was getting for her. She didn't know how she was going to cope for the next three months.

Half an hour later she was sitting in Denver's office ensconced on a comfortable couch with her feet up on the coffee table.

"I can't wait for this child to make its appearance. I feel like a beached whale." Denver rubbed her huge belly and sighed. "Two more weeks and if she doesn't make a start on her own, Frank is going to induce her." She glanced over at

Layla. "Enough about me. Let me see those photos of my nephew." She held out her hand and waited until they were passed over, cooing and smiling at the black and white print.

"He is so cute. Just look at that little nose. Has Tyson seen your scans?"

"No." She bit her lip, willing the tears to stay away and not embarrass herself.

TYSON DID THE buttons up on his shirt and looked in the mirror, checking he'd washed all of the shaving cream off his chin. No point giving his brothers anything to rib him over because they'd take every opportunity. They always did.

Picking up his hat, he headed out of his house and climbed in his truck. He'd missed the friendly dinners but not the accusing looks he got from his family. They only knew what Layla had told them and, it seemed to him, what he said didn't really matter. Not that he let that get to him too much. Rory knew the story and so did Pa. The others could think what they liked, but still it rankled him.

He drove up and parked in front of the big ranch house seconds before Rory pulled in and stopped beside him. He cursed when he saw a strange car. It had to be Layla's. It was small and sporty. The kind a city person would drive. And it was red, a rich, flashy cherry that suited her to a "T". He couldn't very well back out now, not with his brother right there.

Not if he wanted to go through with the appearance of "managing just fine, thank you." Layla was far too observant as it was. Last thing he needed was for her to think he was hankering after her. Besides, he'd known deep down that she would be here and still he agreed to come.

He got out and waited for Rory to join him. "Tyson, nice of you to bother. Thought for minute I'd have to come and give you a hurry up. This was your idea to begin with, if I recall."

"Give me a break, all right? I've had other things on my mind."

"Yeah, but that doesn't mean you were right." He shut his car door and reached into the back seat for a bag.

"Nice to see you, Tyson, even if I think you're being stupid." Gina took Fisher from his car seat before she reached up and kissed Tyson's cheek and handed him the little boy. "Take your nephew while I grab the dinner."

Her belly was huge and he was surprised. It'd been a while since he'd seen her and her baby bump had expanded way more than he thought it should have.

She noticed him gawking. "Yep, big isn't it? Two in there, that's why."

"Two?" He paled at the thought and looked to Rory.

"When I do something, I do it right." Rory winked, seemingly very pleased with what he and Gina had produced. "One of each. We wanted to keep it a surprise for a while but since Gina is so big, we figured we should let everyone know. How's that for perfection?"

Tyson gulped. "Does it hurt?" He couldn't begin to imagine how she was managing.

"Not really. It's getting rather uncomfortable but it's all part and parcel." She laughed as he continued to stare, Fisher resting in his arms. "Here, feel it for yourself, they're moving around." She grabbed his hand and pressed it against her stomach, watching his face.

Tyson tensed, giving Rory a quick glance. His brother stared at him, a huge goofy grin on his face. Then he felt it, the ripple of movement under his hand and then a wave of motion as one of the babies moved and Gina's belly changed shape. He watched as the baby rose and then settled down under his fingers.

"That was, just…"

"Amazing, right?"

"Yeah." His throat tightened and he forced himself to swallow.

It was the first time he'd felt a baby move like that. He was missing this with his own child and the hole it punched in his gut hurt more than anything he could ever remember. There had to be something he could do to change Layla's mind. It was his child she was carrying. He'd never doubted it, not for a moment. But he wanted more. No, he needed more. He wanted a relationship with the mother of his child and, damn it, he was going to get it. Once he figured out how to get over the biggest hurdle.

Her stubbornness. Oh yeah, and that mail-order bride thing. He should have done something about that instead of ignoring it.

Chapter Nine

"I CAN'T BELIEVE how time has flown. You only have three months left, Layla." Callie handed her a glass of water before sitting beside her on the couch. She reached out a hand and rubbed her friend's belly.

Layla grinned up at Chance. "Isn't it time you did something about your wife's penchant for pregnant bellies?"

He smiled indulgently. "Nope. She insists she's not ready. Doesn't mind practicing but the real thing is still some ways off yet. Besides, she gets her fill with you ladies. I really can't believe the three of you are all pregnant at the same time. You wouldn't read about it." Chance leaned on the mantel over the fireplace and watched his wife with a look that bordered on obsessive.

Layla couldn't believe how lucky he had been to find the love of his life with an ad in a cattle magazine. She wished she could follow suit but that didn't seem to be happening no matter how much she might wish it was the truth. Real love evaded her and others had answered the ad she'd placed for Tyson, which only added to her resolve to leave him alone.

True, she'd settled down well in town with her new business. The locals kept her busy enough to stop her mind wandering too much but it was at nighttime when she was in her little rented cottage the loneliness crept in. If only she wasn't too stubborn she would go after what she desperately needed. Things could be a whole lot better if she could get over her pride and talk to Tyson about what she really wanted out of life. Not like her to be so slow in coming forward. The thought of putting in a fake resume for his wife crossed her mind every now and then but common sense prevailed and so far she'd not bothered.

"Yes, well, not like it was planned that way, was it?" She shook of her feeling of impending doom and smiled. "So, how is Denver feeling? I thought they would be here to-night."

Callie laughed. "I did too but Evan called up before and I could hear her in the background yelling at him. She seemed a little bit put out that he cancelled. Claims she is not feeling the best, something about her blood pressure being up and she complained about aches and pains so he's not taking any chances."

"Fair enough. I saw her last week and she was getting pretty antsy being placed on part-time duties." She shook her head, brushing away the hair hanging over her eye. "Must be hard near the end when you can hardly do anything."

Chance looked at her from his position by the fireplace.

"Look, tell me to mind my own business if you want to, but what are you going to do? I mean, are you going to have Tyson with you when the baby is born? I think he'd want to be there."

Layla sighed. "I don't know, Chance."

"Not like you to be unsure of anything, Layla. Since I've known you, you would have to be the most organized, driven person I know."

She laughed, bitterness creeping in. "You've never seen me pregnant and alone before." She reached into her over-sized, bright red handbag and brought out a couple of photos. "Look what I got. The latest pics of the little man. Evan is happy with me and the baby. He seems to be growing well."

Callie tore the photos from her hand and squealed. "He is so cute. Chance, look at that little nose." She uncurled herself from the couch and hurried over to her husband, flashing the photos in front of his face.

"He has the Watson look about him." Chance grinned at Layla and dropped his gaze to the pictures again, taking them from his wife. "Nice strong forehead and that nose, well I guess he'll grow into it."

Callie nudged him in the ribs. "That is just plain mean. It's a cute nose."

Layla leaned back on her cushion and listened to them argue over her unborn son, happy she had at least some support from loved ones. This child wouldn't be lonely. It was only her that would feel that kind of pain.

The door from the front porch slammed and she tensed hearing a voice she knew only too well. The last few family dinners had been easy because he wasn't here. It seemed that tonight he'd had a change of heart about being amongst family. Tyson walked in with Fisher in his arms and stood at the door looking in. "Evening all." He nodded at Layla. "Evening." His cool gaze raked over her and she resisted the urge to squirm. Was it longing she saw behind that stare or was it disdain? Most likely the latter.

She tried to smile but it came off wobbly and Layla looked away trying to gather her wits.

"What's got you two so fired up?" Tyson walked over and looked over Callie's shoulder.

"Um, it's a photo of the baby. Layla's baby." Callie looked over at Layla and mouthed an apology.

She watched Tyson blanch and wished she could reach up and tear the pictures out of Chance's hand.

TYSON HANDED FISHER over to Chance and took the photos from his big brother. The black and white pictures trembled in his hand. This was the child he'd made with Layla after Rory and Gina's wedding. The child he would only be a part-time father to if she got her way. It was easy enough to work out what was what at this stage of the pregnancy. It looked like a baby and he could see the tiny toes and fingers. The baby had what looked like a thumb in its mouth and he felt a softening in his gut and a race of his heart that he couldn't explain even if he tried.

He risked a quick glance at Layla and met her worried gaze before looking back at his child. "Good looking kid." He brushed past Chance and handed her the photos, wishing he could tuck them into his shirt pocket and keep them close to his heart.

"Thanks." She coughed delicately and the strained silence hung heavy in the room.

"I could use a beer, what do you guys want?" Rory walked in and stopped short when he noticed Layla sitting on the couch and Tyson hovering over her. "Hey, Layla. Looking good. Can I get anyone a drink in here?"

Tyson brushed past him back into the kitchen. "I'll get my own." He could hear the whispered voice of Callie consoling Layla but he ignored it and headed to the fridge.

"Tyson, are you okay?" It was Gina and she leaned on the kitchen island watching him, kindness and concern in her eyes.

"Yeah."

"I'm here if you ever need to talk." She put a hand down to rub her belly, screwing up her mouth.

"Are you in pain?" He reached her side, suddenly more concerned about his sister-in-law than his own problems. "Do you want me to get Rory?"

She brushed him off, a tortured smile on her face. "No, no. It's okay really. One of the babies has a knack of digging its heel under my ribs and it hurts. Nothing we can do about it."

He held her arm until she breathed easier and stood straighter. "That was a bad one."

"How do you do it? Put up with all the pain and the morning sickness?"

"It's worth it in the long run. When you get to hold that new life you've made together, all the pain and stress they put you through makes it worth it." She smiled. "I'm sorry you're missing it, Tyson. I really am."

"Me too. I saw a photo just now of my baby. Kind of makes it all the more real, you know?" His heart ached for what he was missing.

"He's such a little cutie, isn't he? I can't wait to meet him."

Him. "Him? I'm getting a son?" How could Gina know and not him?

"You didn't know? Oh no, Tyson, I'm so sorry. I shouldn't be the one to tell you this news." She held her hand up to her mouth, despair in her eyes.

"What have you done to my wife? If you've upset her, you'll have me to answer to." Rory stalked in and glanced between the two of them.

"No, he's done nothing. It's me." Gina looked at her husband. "He didn't know the baby was a boy and tonight is the first time he's seem a photo of the scans."

Rory lifted his hands to his hips and sighed. "Guess tonight will be a good time for you two to talk, don't you think?"

Tyson glanced at him, trying to calm down before he answered.

The hurt burned in his chest. "I can't believe she told you guys and not me. I am the baby's father and I deserve better."

"I think so too. And not because I put my foot in it either. As the father of that child you should have an equal say in things." Gina leaned into her husband, sliding a hand around his waist. "This has gone on long enough. You need to fix whatever it was that made this go all wrong, Tyson. You two had eyes for each other from day one so I don't understand what went so bad between you." She moved from Rory and placed a hand on Tysons back, pushed him toward the living room. "Chance, Callie, can we have you in the kitchen please? These two need some talking time without the family listening in." She gave Tyson a final push and he stumbled into the room, noticing the warning glance his oldest brother shot his way. If he upset her he would have Chance to deal with. *Got it loud and clear but this is nothing to do with you, Chance.*

Once they were on their own, he glanced over at Layla. Her color was high and he thought she looked annoyed or was that cornered to be alone in the room with him? "Hi."

"Hello." She smoothed out the top she was wearing over her bulging stomach.

Tyson wanted to lift it up and touch her belly as he'd done with Gina. He needed to feel his son. "I hear it's a boy."

Her gaze flickered away before settling on the floor in front of her. "Yes."

"You could have told me, Layla. I would rather have heard it from you than my family." He stepped closer. "I know you have all these ideas on how we're going to raise this child but I think I deserve better. I want to be involved, to go to doctor's appointments and see what he has to say. Can't I be there for that at least?"

She looked up, fire in her eyes. "If you'd bothered to call me, I might have told you, Tyson. But since you didn't, you can take the consequences." Her lips tightened to a straight line and her gaze hardened.

"Funnily enough, that works both ways for me. You could have called me too but you didn't. Why not? Why do you have to tell everyone else our business but not me?" He paused a few feet closer in front of her. "Why don't I have any rights all of a sudden?"

"Funny, I thought you would be too busy with your new bride to be to even give us a thought." Her words were like a slap in the face.

"I never—"

"Yes, you did. We discussed this the day I told you I was

pregnant. You professed to love me then but did you cancel the ad or ask me to do it? No, you didn't. So why would I be the one to make all the moves, Tyson? Tell me that one before you get on your high horse and make demands of me."

"Hang on just a minute." Where did she get off being so damned pissed when it was nothing to do with him?

"No, you hang on, cowboy. We're having a child together, no denying it. But damned if I will play meek and mild 'Miss Congeniality' while you get up close and personal with someone else. You want this child in your life, you can make the effort. After all, I'm the one who turned her life upside down to come here so the baby can get to know its family, even when its father was looking for another woman. I could just as well as stayed put and told you nothing."

"And you seem to be forgetting I'm the one you ignored once you'd had your roll in the hay with a cowboy. Seems I was good enough for sex but nothing else." Tyson stood with his hands on his hips, staring down at her while his heart pumped in his chest.

He was furious she wanted to lay all the blame on his shoulders.

She pushed herself to her feet and looked up into his eyes. "Cast your mind back. The weekend of the wedding, with me on this?" Her snappy lawyer mode was creeping back in and he flinched and nodded his head knowing it would be better top let her get it out of her system.

"Do you remember what you said when I left on the last day to fly back out?"

Stay with me, or that was awesome sex, I can't wait to do it again. Hell, no I don't. "Not exactly word for word, no."

"Well, I do." She leaned in, pointed her finger into his chest and poked it into his flesh, hard. "Thanks for the best weekend I've had for ages." She poked again, her finger not quite so hard this time. "Not when can we do it again or can I call you. Oh no, happy to have me in your bed for the weekend but that's all you wanted, plain and simple."

"No it wasn't—"

"Yes, it was. Let's face it, if you cared, you would have made the effort but you didn't. You let me walk away with no hint of us being together in the future. I got on that plane home feeling like a freaking call girl who you'd forget as soon as she walked out the damned door. But that's not really the issue here, merely an added insult. We are from two totally different backgrounds, Tyson. How long do you think it will be before you get annoyed with me for being too clever or too rich?" She stepped back and crossed her arms over her baby bump, glaring at him. "Not very long, I can assure you. I had a relationship once, fell in love with a young man I had every intention of marrying. He was from another country – no big deal. Different lifestyle – no big deal. Until he announced to his family he wanted to marry me. Things got nasty and suddenly he couldn't wait to go back to his own country and marry someone 'appropriate.' I made the decision then to stick to my own kind of person, rash or not, that is what I did and I can't go against that and get hurt all over again."

"So, I was just a roll in the hay to you, someone to scratch an itch. You had no intention of making it more than that. You just admitted it."

"I pursued you, I admit that but I thought maybe I was being too hard, maybe there was something between us regardless of my earlier beliefs. I guess I was wrong and when Chance asked me to take care of your 'mail-order bride business,' I realized how wrong I was. You don't have to try and make me feel better. I enjoyed it too while it lasted but we got caught out so now we have to deal with the consequences the best way we can." Her chest heaved after the outburst.

"But I never wanted—"

"I'm sorry I didn't tell you more about the baby but I didn't think you cared. Obviously you had other things on your mind." She lifted a finger and wiped it under her eye. Tyson reached for her but she stepped out of reach. "Don't worry about me, I'm fine. And I'll make sure I tell you how the baby is in future, that's if it's what you want."

"Of course I want to know what's going on. He's my son. I don't want to hear it all from my family." The words to convince her drifted away, the opportunity fading away under her icy stare.

Layla leaned down and took a photo from her handbag.

"I got copies in case you might want to have one." She handed it over and he gladly took it.

"Thank you." He ran a finger around the black and white shape, his heart doing all manner of flips and starts in his chest. "So everything is okay? You're feeling good?"

Her glance softened and she cleared her throat before answering. "Yes. Evan is happy with me so far."

"Make sure you call me if you need anything, okay?" He slid the photo in his shirt pocket. "I want to be there for you, Layla. I want to be at the next doctor's visit. I want what other fathers have." *I want to be there when my baby comes into the world.*

"Too late, Tyson. Much too late."

Chapter Ten

LAYLA DID HER best to appear upbeat and unaffected with Tyson sitting next to her at the dinner table. They'd agreed to put on a brave face for the sake of the family lest they get pressured to kiss and make-up. She made the suggestion lightly, striving for a dismissive attitude as if it didn't wound her to be in the same room as the man she still lusted after. He hadn't told her she had it wrong either, which was the kicker as far as she was concerned. Oh yes, he'd attempted to protest but to her it was no more than a weak attempt, which he never backed up. And she noticed he hadn't said anything about getting married either. Layla was too proud to ask Chance and there was no way she'd ask Tyson which of the applicants he preferred. Heaven forbid he think she still cared. *Give a girl some pride.*

Used to people throwing platitudes her way in her career to get off the latest charges laid against them, Layla wanted more than half-assed attempts to fob her off. She wanted a man who would fight for her through thick and thin when times got hard and still love her while he did it, even if he

ANN B. HARRISON

came out the other side scratched and bruised. For a while, she'd thought Tyson might be that man but it didn't appear to be so. She kicked herself mentally. Normally such a good judge of character, she'd made a monumental blunder and it irked on a very deep level.

Chance finished carving the meat and placed the big platter in the middle of the table.

Rory sniffed appreciatively and smiled. "Can't beat a decent piece of beef. Looks like you've done yourself proud, Callie."

She blushed and giggled. "Thank your father. He put it on for me before he went home tonight. Something about secret marinades and herbs."

"Where is the old man? Surprised to see him missing." Tyson speared himself a piece of meat before holding the platter out to Layla. She took a small piece and thanked him, keeping her voice neutral.

"Reckons he had a date. Wouldn't say who though and I asked him point blank too. Sneaky little guy is stepping out by the look of it." She laughed and passed the vegetables over to Tyson. He held the bowl while Layla helped herself.

"About time he made the move on her. Been skirting around each other for years."

"Who are you talking about?" Chance pinned his littlest brother with a look over the table.

"Milly Forester. You remember the lady couple of houses down from us? Used to tan our hides when we were kids when we got into mischief. She's always had a soft spot for Pa and I wish them well. Everyone needs someone."

While the family nodded in agreement with Tyson, Layla froze beside him. He'd made the comment in relation to his father. But did the underlying meaning suggest he'd liked what she'd forwarded to him? Did that mean he was already in the throes of arranging his marriage.

"Layla, are you feeling alright?" Gina watched her over the dinner table.

"Yes, fine. A little tired maybe but that's all." She picked up her knife and fork and cut the meat, taking a small bite as everyone watched her. She chewed and swallowed, doing her best to appear fine. "Stop worrying. There's nothing wrong with me, I promise. An early night might be on the cards I think though."

"I know how you feel." Gina rubbed her belly and sighed. "Only problem I have is as soon as I lay down, the twins wake up and think it's time to party. Makes bedtime seem like torture."

"And you wonder why I'm happy to wait." Callie picked up her glass of wine and took a sip making exaggerated slurping noises. "Besides, who could give up such nice wine for early morning vomits and sore backs? Not this little black duck."

"Little black duck. Where on earth did that come from?" Chance peered at his wife.

"Aussie slang, sorry."

"You sure do come up with some interesting stuff." He smiled at her affectionately and Callie winked at him.

TYSON KEPT WATCH on her from the corner of his eye. She was definitely on tenterhooks with him sitting beside her. *That had to mean something, right?*

The phone shrilled, breaking the mood around the table. Chance got up to answer it, leaning against the kitchen counter with the phone clutched to his ear. Tyson kept a watch on him while trying to engage Layla in conversation.

"That was Evan. He's taken Denver in. Apparently she's having contractions and he doesn't want to take any chances."

"Oh, I knew she was feeling off today." Gina grabbed Rory's arm. "This is going to be so emotional. I can't wait to meet the little person." Her eyes misted over and Rory put his arm around her shoulders.

"Does he want anyone to come and keep him company?" Callie looked at Chance as he took a seat back at the table.

"I think that'd be a good idea. He sounded pretty stressed out. Who wants to go and sit with them?"

"I do." Gina was the first to speak.

"No. I don't think that's a good idea." Rory was shaking his head even as she started to protest. "You're already dead on your feet. If I'd had my way, we wouldn't be here tonight, you'd be in bed resting."

"You should listen to him, Gina. This pregnancy is taking its toll on you. Twins are draining you more than I think even you expected." Callie reached a hand over the table and gripped her friend's fingers for a quick squeeze. "How about Chance and I go up and I keep you posted via cell phone messages and I might even send you a couple of photos, okay?"

"She's right, Gina. I'm taking you home straight after dinner for a rest." Rory kissed his wife and smiled at his sister-in-law. "Thanks Callie. This wife of mine thinks she can do so much but I think we know better now." He dropped another kiss on her temple as she smiled weakly.

"Right, let's eat and then we can go and help Evan get through this." Chance picked up his fork and stabbed a piece of meat.

Chapter Eleven

TYSON SAW THE wariness in Layla's eyes when Chance and Callie hurried from the house, promising to keep them all informed of developments at the hospital.

"I guess I'd better get you home too, my love." Rory winked at Gina who had given into her tiredness and yawned all through dinner. She sat rubbing her belly, shadows under her eyes.

"I really wanted to go to the hospital and be there for Denver."

"I know but it's not going to happen on my watch and Callie did say she'd keep you posted. Pretty sure your doctor wouldn't be happy to see you there. Think he'll have enough on his plate to deal with." He ran a finger down her cheek. "How about if I take you in first thing in the morning. We can drop Fisher off at Dad's for an hour."

Gina nodded her head and once again Tyson envied his brother the love he'd found.

"Or you can bring him over to me for a bit. About time I got the chance to look after him." He stood up, pushed back his chair and startled Fisher who screwed up his face and started to cry. "Sorry, little buddy. Your mom isn't the only one looking tired and ready for bed." He reached over and picked him up, leaning him against his shoulder. Fisher sighed and closed his eyes, popping his thumb in his mouth. "You guys go home. I'll clear up the dishes here before I leave."

"I'll help. Just get Gina home, Rory, before she falls in a heap." Layla smiled at her friend and Tyson shared a glance with his brother. *It would be another chance to talk to her.* He could read that message in Rory's glance but Tyson doubted she'd be willing. He should be grateful she was prepared to be civil after what he'd put her through.

They helped get the family into their truck. Fisher never stirred when Tyson belted him into his car seat. "Looks like the littlest cowboy is worn out."

"He'll sleep all night. Had a very big day." Rory tooted the horn as they drove down the driveway, the taillights winking in the darkness.

Tyson turned to Layla. "You don't have to stay. I can do the dishes."

"No, it's okay. I don't mind, we have to get used to being around each other, Tyson." She turned from him and walked back indoors, started to stack and collect the plates from the table.

Tyson followed, determined to give it another try now there was nobody to overhear them. Perhaps Layla would be more open to a discussion when none of the family were around.

First, he picked up the tea towel ready to help while choosing his words. Layla filled the sink with hot water, squirted in the dishwashing liquid and started on the plates. Tyson watched her top cling to the baby bump as she worked, fascinated that his child was growing inside her body.

"Is there a problem?"

He glanced up at her face and couldn't tell if she was annoyed or amused by his concentration. "Uh, no. Sorry but this is all kind of new to me and I'm...

"Appalled, annoyed, pissed off you can't break me like you can your damned horses?" She fumed and if he was a wise man he'd let it go and walk away.

But Tyson wasn't one for giving up and decided if he didn't try now, he'd never get another opportunity. "No! Never. What is it going to take to get you to understand, Layla? I didn't think Chance was going to put that ad in the paper. I only wrote it because I was drunk and hurting after you left." He shuffled his feet, knowing now would be a good time to stop pressuring her. Slow steps rather than rushing in always worked better in his opinion. "I should have taken it out of the paper but I chose to ignore it instead, thinking it might go away. Besides, you're right. I have nothing to offer you and we come from such different backgrounds."

SHE THREW THE dish brush in the sink, spraying water up over her shirt. Her own words were coming back to bite her and she hated it. *Nothing to offer her – what an idiot!*

"You lived in the city, drive an expensive car, and have more money dripping from your fingertips than I'll ever know. Why on earth would you think we could have more than what we had?"

Layla could feel her blood pressure rising and it took all of her hard learned skills to not strike out at him. He was even more stubborn than any prosecutor she'd ever met in the courtroom.

"You should maybe stop while you're ahead, Tyson. Don't go saying something you can't take back." She rested her soapy hands on the edge of the counter, breathing steadily.

"It's too late. I wish I could take back what I said when you told me you were pregnant but I can't. If I was one of those swank guys you deal with every day in your business, would I have said the wrong thing? I doubt it. I'd probably have wooed you with flowers and fine dining not dragged you back to my rundown ranch and—"

"Made love to me like no one else has before? Blew my mind enough that I didn't want to leave when Sunday came around? Cried on the plane because I didn't want to leave you? Yeah, that did it for me, Tyson. But it wasn't enough for you to make a phone call to see if we could do it again, to try and change my idea of what a good relationship needed. Is it any wonder I want to stick to my resolve about our differences? So how about you stop telling me how much I don't want someone like you."

She met his gaze and saw the uncertainty there but would it be enough for her to give in and make a fool of herself again if he didn't tell her what she wanted to hear?

"I can't offer you what you want, Layla." He lifted his hand to her cheek and then dropped it.

She swallowed. "You haven't even asked me what I want, so how could you possibly know?" A flutter under her ribs distracted her and Layla lifted a hand to her stomach.

The baby was awake.

"What is it? Is there something wrong? Layla, talk to me, damn it!" Tyson had his hands on her arms, his face bare inches from hers. The panic in his eyes jolted her out of her wonder.

"The baby. It moved."

He softened the grip on her arms, dropped his hands. "Moved?"

She took one of his hands and put it on her stomach just as the flutter spread over the front of her belly again. "Feel that?"

Tyson's eyes glazed over and his mouth dropped open. "I'm not sure. It was so quick and faint."

"Well, that was our baby making his presence known."

"Really?" Tyson cleared his throat before he spoke again. "Thank you for letting me feel that." He gazed into her eyes and she was desperate to know what he really thought. "I want what's best for our baby, Layla, and I wish it was both of us together but I don't think it will work as much as I'd like to think otherwise. Just let me be there for you, okay? Don't shut me out."

Layla swallowed the tears that crept up her throat. She'd made the call and now just when she thought he would fight her on it and tell her what she wanted to hear, Tyson agreed. She was gutted.

Layla swallowed hard and pulled herself together. "Let's get this place cleaned up and then I need to head for home. I've had a long day."

Tyson picked up the tea towel again and grabbed a plate, drying it before placing it on the counter. "So, how is it going, working in such a small town compared to the big city? Finding enough to keep you busy?"

She dropped her shaking hands into the water and picked up the brush again. He did playing the nothing is wrong game well.

She wished she could carry it off as easily. "Sure. More family wills and small stuff like that. Only a couple of court appearances so far but that suits me. I don't want the big workload I had in Denver."

"What are you going to do when the baby comes? How will you manage work then?"

"I don't know, haven't really thought about it, to be honest. I'm still kind of finding my feet." *And wishing for things I can't have.*

Chapter Twelve

RORY PULLED UP at Tyson's place early the next morning while he was standing out on the porch with his first cup of coffee in his hand. He put his mug on the ground, walked down, and opened the back door of the truck where Fisher looked up at him expectantly, his little hands reaching for his uncle. "So, little man. You and me, eh?" He undid the safety harness and lifted the little boy from the seat.

"How're Denver and Evan?"

Gina poked her head out the window. "Happy but tired. Their little girl didn't arrive until 2:30 this morning but she's healthy, so that's the main thing. Are you sure you're going to be alright with Fisher? He's getting kind of active and will be off exploring if you turn your back on him."

Rory passed out an oversized bag which he knew would hold everything the boy could possibly need. Gina was nothing if not organized.

"We'll be fine. I have plenty to do around the yard this morning anyway. He can help me." Tyson watched Fisher heading to the stables and turned to follow him. "See you later."

"There's snacks and clean clothes in the bag. I won't be too long, Tyson. Thank you." Gina waved as they drove away.

"Right, Fisher. Let me tell you the rules, little guy." Tyson hurried off after the child, catching up to him as he rounded the barn door. "No going in the stables with the horses and don't head off without telling me, okay?" Fisher looked at him with a grin on his face. "If you get hungry, shout out 'cause I know your momma packed enough to feed the pair of us and, between us, we're going to work up an appetite. I waited for you to arrive before I started the chores."

Together they fed the horses, cleaned out the stables, and collected eggs from the motely bunch of chickens that spent their days scratching around the stables and barn. Tyson and Fisher were busy sharing finger-sized sandwiches, sitting on a bale of hay together when Gina walked into the barn.

"Just look at you two. I hope he hasn't been too much bother, Tyson." She waddled over and took a seat next to then, ruffling her little boy's hair.

"Not a bother. It was good to have him around, you know. Kind of give me an idea of what I might be up for."

"I wish I could say something to make that easier for you but at least you two are talking about it."

"Thank goodness for small mercies."

Fisher jumped down and ran across the barn when he

heard a chicken clucking. "Oh dear, he knows that sound only too well. Always running out and getting the chickens off the nest to take the eggs."

"He's a great kid, Gina."

"Yes, he is and he'll make a wonderful big brother." She smiled whimsically, then looked at him. "Oh, I almost forgot. I took some photos to show you of the new baby. I sent them to Layla to see but since you don't have a mobile phone of your own, I promised Evan I'd show you these." She pulled her phone from her pocket and pressed a few buttons before handing it over to Tyson. "Slide your finger across the screen to see the others. Isn't she gorgeous?"

Tyson took the phone and glanced at the tiny baby. Her face was wrinkled and bright pink and he almost said so before biting his tongue. "She's, uh, pretty." He swiped across to the next photo and it was Denver, Evan, and the baby. His brother and wife looked exhausted but happy.

"She's a bit squished but that will change in a week or so. Then she'll be really pretty."

Fisher cried out, a chicken squawked and came flying out of a pile of hay bales, ruffled feathers fluttering as she clucked and protested the disturbance. The little boy followed with an egg in his hand, the triumphant hunter gatherer. Tears poured down his cheeks as he ran toward them.

Before Gina could get up, Tyson reached for him and picked him up. "What happened little buddy? That chicken wanted to keep her egg to herself, did she?"

The bottom lip quivered before a small sound came out.

He held the egg up to show Tyson. "Mine."

Tyson laughed and ruffled Fisher's hair. "You take that egg home and have it for lunch." He carried him over to Gina. "You look pretty tired still, want me to put this little one in his car seat for you?"

"Thanks, Tyson, appreciate it. When he goes down for his afternoon nap, I think I'll do the same. Funny but I wasn't as tired this early with Fisher."

"Must make a difference with the two of them I'm guessing." He cleared his throat. "I mean, not that I know or anything but it stands to reason I think."

Gina smiled and patted him on the arm. "You're right, that's what I put it down to as well. Heaven help me in a couple of months when I'm the size of a house. I won't be able to walk or chase after this little guy." She smoothed her son's hair then wiped a finger over his cheeks to dry off his tears.

"You can always drop him over here if you need to. I think we get on pretty well now and I can always find something to keep him occupied."

"That's sweet of you. Thanks."

Tyson walked her out to the truck "I mean it, Gina. Let me know if you need a hand. I'm more than happy to have Fisher hang out with me when you need a break. We're tight, aren't we, little cowboy?" He strapped Fisher in the back of the truck and shut the door before walking over to peer through the driver's open window. "I'll tell Rory too, Gina. Call me when you need anything."

She raised an eyebrow at him.

"Alright. I'll check the answering machine more often but I mean it. He's no trouble and I still get my work done. I like having a little sidekick around and you need more rest." He promised himself he would check it at least twice a day. Now he'd made the offer, he could hardly ignore the stupid contraption. "I love him too."

"I know you do. Thanks."

He watched her drive away before heading back to his horses. He had new shoes to fit that he couldn't do with the boy around and after lunch he'd decided he'd go and ride the trail again to make sure it was safe enough for beginners before he put the sign on the gate that stated he was open for business. Pa had painted signs and arrows that clearly marked the trails he'd worked out. Everything was ready apart from his slight bundle of nerves. He had to get started sooner or later. Might as well make it now.

Might even head into town and put an ad in the local paper too. Casually walk past Layla's office and make sure she was okay. Not that she'd thank him for doing it but Tyson couldn't keep away, not now he'd seen and felt his son move under his mother's skin.

Chapter Thirteen

LAYLA HEARD THE front door of the office slam and winced. Emily's raised voice made Layla lift her head from the papers she was busy reading, a sense that something was wrong. She pushed her chair back and stood up ready to go and see who had upset her receptionist. Her door flew open and one of the Hansen boys stood in the doorway, his face twisted in anger. Layla refused to back down and walked around to the front of her desk. They'd never met although he was the spitting image of his grandfather, Rupert.

"Now, see here. I don't appreciate you putting ideas into an old man's head." He lifted his hand and poked his finger near her face to make a point.

"Sit down." Layla indicated a chair.

"This ain't a social visit, Ms. High Flying City Lawyer. You told Grandpa to change his will, didn't you?"

Layla leaned against her desk, crossed her hands over her stomach. "I think that should come under client lawyer information, don't you? Which, if you didn't understand the term, means it's privileged information that I will not share with you as you are not my client." Emily hovered in the doorway and Layla smiled reassuringly at her. "Thanks, Emily, I'm sure Mr. Hansen is just leaving since he doesn't have an appointment."

"I ain't going anywhere until you tell me what I want to know so she can go back to her desk and keep her nose outta my business."

He glared at Emily and she stuck her chin up. "Your grandpa will have a fit to bust if he could see you now, Jethro. That's no way to speak to a lady."

"Some lady. Getting herself knocked up with a dirt poor cowboy who has to rely on his big brother for handouts." He turned back to Layla and looked her up and down, a sneer on his mouth.

It was the first time anyone had gazed at her like that and it hurt in more ways than one.

"I don't believe my life was the topic of conversation here. Now, if you wish to make an appointment, might I suggest you leave and do so on your way out?" She felt a small pang of pain for her baby and the small-minded comments that had wounded her.

"Right. You think I'd want to pay for the privilege of discussing my Grandpa's will with the likes of you? I don't think so. I'm sure what I suspect is true though, you've turned him against the only family he has left."

"I think you and your brothers did that all by yourselves, Jethro. Gave the man hell ever since your poor mother passed away. And what did he do to deserve such rotten behavior?" Emily walked further into the office.

"If you two think you can take what's rightfully ours, you got another thing coming. That ranch belongs to me and my brothers when Grandpa passes on and if it don't stay that way, I'll be after your hide. You hear me, fancy city lawyer?" His gaze dropped to her chest and stayed there.

A noise came from the reception room and Emily stepped to one side as Tyson barged into the office, a look of thunder on his face. *How much had he heard?*

Layla put her hand up to stop him but he ignored her and grabbed Jethro by the throat. "You're coming with me."

"Tyson, don't, please. This isn't the way to deal with him. I'd prefer to do things properly."

He glanced at her and shook his head. "Nobody talks to the mother of my child like that. Not now, not ever. Especially not this scumbag." He turned Jethro around with his hand behind his back and marched him out of the office.

"Emily, call Rory." Layla held a hand over her stomach and followed out to the reception room, trying to keep her eyes on Tyson.

"Already on it." She picked up the phone. "You stay out of the way now, you hear? Those two have been at each other's throats since they were in diapers. Just can't help themselves. Not that Jethro doesn't deserve it this time but still, Rory won't like Tyson getting into trouble again."

Layla looked out the window into the street. The two

men were facing each other, words flying and fists gesturing to the office and back. "They're going to kill each other unless I do something." She opened the door ignoring Emily's cry of protest.

Jethro shouted a profanity and swung his closed fist, connecting with the side of Tyson's head. Tyson staggered back with the blow but came right back with a right hook of his own. Layla yelled at them but they didn't hear or chose to ignore her.

"Bloody hell, you two, stop it. Now!" She pushed her way between them, intent on drawing them apart. Jethro caught her on the side of the face with a closed fist. She looked at him in disbelief. Never in all of her years in the courtroom had she been hurt, even by the roughest of her clients. The stars floating in front of her eyes made Tyson's next punch to Jethro's face seem almost comical, in slow motion. She slid boneless to the ground.

"LAYLA." TYSON IGNORED the crumpled figure of his school yard frenemy, lying in the road and dropped to his knees beside Layla. Her cheekbone shone with a red mark where Jethro's punch had landed and he could already see the swelling coming up.

"Layla, honey. Open your eyes." He slid his hands under her legs and shoulders and lifted her up into his arms. Her head lolled against his shirt.

"Bring her inside. Rory is on the way, he can deal with Jethro." Emily held open the door and he hurried inside under her disapproving gaze. With nowhere to lay her down, Tyson sat on a chair in the reception area and held Layla on his knee, her face on his chest, stroking her hair while willing her to wake up. She was the one who always knew what she was doing, a tough and go get 'em kind of person. To see her like this didn't seem right and it was his fault.

Emily hurried over to him with a damp cloth in her hand. "Put this on her forehead. Should help some."

Tyson took it and placed the cold cloth on Layla's head, stroking her bangs out of the way. She stirred and tried to push the cloth away.

"Leave it there, honey. Shhh, don't fight me, please." Her eyes fluttered and closed before a hand went to her stomach, swiping it around the pronounced mound.

If anything happens to my son, Jethro will die. You might not want me, Layla, but I will protect you and our baby, I promise. It's the least I can give you.

Her hand went up to her cheek and she winced when her fingers touched the swelling. "Ouch, that hurts."

Tyson could see the tears welling in her eyes and that hurt him more than anything. "I think I should take you in to see Evan. Make sure you're okay and then I'm going to take a visit to the Hansen's ranch. I'll make sure those damned boys never hurt you again."

Layla's hand went to her mouth and she bolted off his knee and staggered toward the bathroom. He glanced at Emily undecided what to do, stood up clutching the damp cloth in his hand. She shrugged her shoulders and looked at the door. They could both hear the retching sound from where they stood.

He hurried over and tapped on the door. "Layla, let me help you." The only response he got was a gagging noise followed by a groan. Tyson opened the door and found her sitting on the floor with her head over the toilet bowl. He crouched down beside her in the small space and tucked a strand of pale hair behind her ear.

When she flicked him a glance, he could see the tears still there. Tyson lifted up the damp cloth and wiped her face, catching the tears and the sweat rolling down her temples.

"Not so pretty this end of things, is it?" She swallowed and grabbed the cloth from him, pushing it against her lips.

"No, but if it's all part and parcel of having a baby, not a lot you can do about it. Not unless Evan has come up with some kind of wonder drug for morning sickness." He paused a moment, a horrible thought racing through his brain. "This is from morning sickness, isn't it? Nothing to do with that fist hitting you in the face?" The anger quickly welled in his chest to replace the anxiousness that had swamped him seconds before.

"Stop! You can't do this, Tyson. You can't go punching anyone that annoys you."

"Annoys me? It was more than that and you know it, Layla. He was rude to you and made uncalled for comments about the two of us. Bloody fool, his mouth always did run off and get him into trouble." He stood up and reached down to slip his hands under her arms helping her to her feet. "I know I'm dirt poor but that doesn't give him license to talk about you like that. Boy needs to watch his tongue around women."

He walked her out of the bathroom and back to the chair she'd moments ago bolted from. They could see a commotion out the front window. Rory had picked up Jethro from the road and they stood arguing. Jethro pointed his clenched fist in their direction. "Best I go and sort this out."

"Best if you take Layla over to Evan and get her checked out first." Emily glowered at him, her lips tight. "You can deal with the deputy later."

"I'm fine." She hung her head over her hands, hiding her face from him.

"Mrs. Forsythe is right. You need to be checked over. Come on." He hooked a hand through her arm and walked her out the door holding his hand up when Rory started toward him.

"Layla needs to see Evan before anything else. Pretty sure Jethro can tell you about how he knocked her down with a fist to her face. I'd be happy to charge him with assault if it was up to me." He walked her to his truck and helped her into the front seat, ignoring her protests.

"Hey, not fair. I didn't mean to, she got in the way. I was aiming for your fat head." Jethro tried to get his point across but nobody seemed to care right now.

Tyson shut the door and turned to Rory. "I'll be back later. Then we'll sort this idiot out. In the meantime, a cooling off period might be in order. Pretty sure you'll have an empty cell with his name on it. If you don't, you should with all the damned trouble him and his brothers have caused."

Chapter Fourteen

LAYLA LAY BACK and let Evan check her vital signs. Having Tyson holding her hand was an unfamiliar sensation and one she could get used to but she knew better than to even think about it. He was being kind because he felt responsible, nothing more. She withdrew her fingers and pretended the action was so she could touch the swelling on her cheek.

"That's going to be very pretty shades of black before the end of the day." Evan frowned and put the stethoscope on her belly to listen to the baby. "Sounds all good to me."

"Don't you need to do an x-ray or something, make sure he's really okay?" Tyson stood at the head of the bed watching every move his brother made.

"Nope. Baby is fine, I promise. How's the morning sickness, Layla?"

"Morning, noon, and night you mean. Not letting up much actually." Having Tyson wipe her face when she was vomiting over the toilet bowl had made it all seem so much easier but that wouldn't be happening again anytime soon.

Not if she could help it anyway. As much as she wanted him there, it would only lead to heartache and that wasn't in the plan. He wasn't interested in her that way and she more than anyone knew that.

"Nothing I can give you at this stage, I'm afraid. Make sure you drink plenty of fluids of course and rest up as much as you can. It should ease off soon, in fact in most cases it would be done with by now. You must be a special case."

"Of course she is. Any fool can see that."

Layla breathed in slowly, letting the breath out before turning to Tyson. "You need to stop being so overprotective, Tyson. I understand, really I do but there's no need to be ridiculous about this."

"Ridiculous? You got punched in the face by that idiot and you think I'm being ridiculous?" He stood up, hands on hips as he paced the small room.

Evan stood where he was, looking between the two of them.

"If you hadn't dragged him outside, none of this would have happened. I deal with unhappy clients all the time, it's part of my job." Layla pushed herself up into a sitting position and gave Evan a sympathetic look then stopped worrying about it. Surely he knew his little brother and his moods by now. "If things had gotten out of hand I would have called Rory and pressed charges. Simple, but I doubt he would have hit me if you weren't there stirring things up."

"He all but called you a loose woman because you're having a poor man's baby. I don't care what he says about me but there is no way I'm letting him get away with talking down to you like that. He deserved more than he got." Tyson's eyes darkened.

"If you knew me at all, you'd know how much I hate violence and like to uphold the law, considering it's my job and all. I don't need you standing up for me and making a mockery of my principles, Tyson."

"But I have every right to protect you. Evan, tell her." He turned to his brother for help.

All Evan did was hold out his hands.

Layla pounced. "Don't go dragging your brother into this, it's our problem not his. I need the town to see me as a law-abiding, upstanding citizen, Tyson. Not someone who has a man bashing anyone who upsets her. As far as I'm concerned, you've already tarnished that reputation. I'm not happy, let me tell you that much."

"You're crazy. All I did was defend what's mine."

"Now there's the mistake you're making. This baby might be yours, but I'm not. You've made your position clear so let's leave it at that." Layla averted her head but not before she saw the hurt in his eyes. "Don't worry about getting me back to the office, I'll walk. You must have things to do at the ranch." She schooled her face and looked up at him unprepared for the depth of pain in his eyes.

Tyson looked briefly at Evan before storming out of the examination room.

"That was a bit harsh, don't you think?"

Layla blushed, the heat racing up her cheeks. "I had no choice, Evan. He's acting all macho like it's okay to bash someone for letting off steam. I can't have him throwing his weight around, especially at my place of work."

"I get that but don't you think the two of you should sort out what's really going on here? We both know this isn't what's bothering you the most." He stood watching her, no doubt waiting for her to confess and open her heart to him but Layla couldn't do it, no matter how understanding Evan was.

He was a Watson boy and they all stuck together, even if they didn't think that was how they worked. Tyson might have been the butt of their jokes growing up but when push came to shove, he was still their little brother and blood always shone through.

"We've talked and agreed to both bring up this baby. That is where we're at and I'm happy with that arrangement." *And I don't know how much you know about his other arrangements. Not my place to fill you in either.* She swung her legs over the edge of the bed, raising a hand to her sore face. "Anything I can do to make this look better? Don't want to have to explain it to everyone I see."

"Not really. You could ice it but it's still going to give you a black eye and a pretty-colored bruise for the next few weeks. Besides, being a small town everyone will probably know what happened by now anyway. Are you going to press charges?"

She looked at him, horrified he'd think that way. "No. There's no point when I was the one who got in the way."

"Might I suggest then, that you refrain from 'getting in the way' of two big-headed idiots that have been tripping over each other with fists flying since kindergarten? They'll never see eye to eye over anything and you're only asking for trouble trying to pull them apart. Do what we did, Layla. Let them go for it until they've had enough and stay out of the firing range." Evan held out his hand and helped her down from the bed.

"Thanks, Evan."

"Might I also suggest you go home and put your feet up? Not the kind of excitement I normally suggest for my mothers to be."

"I would but with such short days already I have clients to see to. But don't worry about me, I'll be sensible. Besides, Emily watches over me like a hawk thanks to Chance."

"Well, she failed in this instance, didn't she? And you're not walking back to the office. Have her come and pick you up."

TYSON STORMED INTO the sheriff's department and headed straight to Rory's office. He pushed the door open without knocking and barged inside. Rupert Hansen sat in front of his brother.

"Don't you know how to knock?" Rory glanced up, a steely glare on his face. "This isn't a damned barn, Tyson."

"Sorry. Didn't mean to interrupt. My apologies Mr. Hansen. I'll wait outside."

Rupert pushed himself to his feet and held up a hand. "No, stay. This concerns you as well, I guess, after that damned stunt Jethro pulled today."

Tyson glanced at his brother and waited for the nod before he shut the door and took position, leaning against the wall beside the water cooler.

Rupert sat back down and sighed. "I'm sorry about what happened, Tyson. Ms. Cox is a lovely woman and didn't deserve that mouthful my grandson gave her. She was only doing what I asked." He coughed and pulled a handkerchief from his pocket, dabbed it at his eyes.

Tyson shared a look with Rory.

"The thing is, none of the boys are taking this well. Doc hasn't given me much time and I wanted to sort things out so they don't ruin everything I've worked so hard for. They might be rough and stupid sometimes but they're my grandsons and all I have left. Layla and I talked it over and, to protect the ranch, I changed my will. I told them today over breakfast what I'd done. They didn't like it, as you can imagine, even though I refused to tell them the finer details. Guessing they're thinking the worst and so they should be too." He sniffled. "If they had their way they'd drink and gamble it all 'til there was nothing left and I didn't spend all my life working for that to happen."

"Still no reason to go and take it out on her like that." Tyson couldn't keep the venom out of his voice.

"I agree and that's why Jethro is sitting out back in a cell for a bit." Rory sat forward. "Now, if I was a fair man, which I like to think I am, you'd be joining him for disturbing the peace."

"What?" Tyson pushed himself from the wall.

"But, Rupert has asked me not to press charges against you and therefore, you can calm down. Layla may want to though, I'll have to wait and see what she says when I catch up with her later."

"Good luck with that. All but told me to mind my own business." The conversation rolled over in his mind and Tyson experienced the hurt all over again. *Not his woman! And whose fault was that?* He'd tried, but perhaps not hard enough.

"Well, far be it to give advice where it's not wanted but, in my experience, the longer you leave things the harder it is to fix 'em." Rupert looked up at him from under salt and pepper, bushy eyebrows. "Seems to me that little lady got into the condition she is because you two had something in common. Would hate to think you were as fickle as my boys." He heaved himself to his feet. "Let Jethro stew in there for another few hours before you let him loose, Rory. Sure as hell won't hurt him none."

Tyson held the door for the old man and watched him walk out.

"So she's pretty annoyed at you from what I can gather then?" Rory sat back down at his desk and watched his little brother shut the door and take a seat.

"Yeah, pretty much. Told me it's not my business and I've lowered her status in the community or some such crap." He ran a hand over his head, anger building again.

Rory grinned. "She does have her reputation to uphold. I guess that's pretty important to her."

"But he mouthed off at her. Called her a cheap woman who got knocked up by a poor cowboy. Did you expect me to stand there and take that?" He glared at his brother, daring him to disagree. "I don't care what he calls me, I can deal with that." He swallowed.

He was poor and wouldn't have the ranch without Chance's help but he wasn't cheap and he liked to think he worked harder than some. Sure as hell worked harder than any of the Hansen boys and they knew it.

"But to talk about Layla like that, it isn't right."

"No, it isn't and I agree. But Tyson, dragging him out on the street and punching him in front of her place of business wasn't a good idea. Hell, if you wanted to have a go at the guy, least you could have done was take him out the back door where there were less people to see your carrying on."

Tyson looked across the desk and noticed the way his

brother's lips twitched. It was nice to know he wasn't in that much trouble, at least with Rory.

"But, on another note, don't go thinking I agree with you that this solves a problem. It doesn't and I think you know that."

"Sure as heck made me feel better until he hit Layla on the face though."

"Is she alright?" Rory leaned back and crossed his hands across his chest.

"Far as Evan is concerned, yeah. Going to have a great shiner though and I figure that's going to annoy her."

"And you?"

"I've tried. Lord knows I've tried but she won't listen to me. Agrees we can bring up our son together but not together if you know what I mean. I don't know if that's going to work for us but at the moment it's the only option she's giving me."

"Still don't understand what the problem is or why you'd even consider the idea of finding someone else."

"I didn't call her after the wedding, placed an ad for a bride, and she has thing about us being too different. I said the wrong thing too when she left apparently but, think about it, Rory, I don't have enough to offer her anyway so maybe it's for the best."

"You need to stop selling yourself short. Bet there are plenty of girls out there who would love to marry a self-made man like you."

Tyson snorted in disbelief. "Yeah, right. Like I can see

them lining up." He ran a hand over his head. "All I want is Layla and our son but it's not going to happen." Tyson looked toward the door. "Well, since you aren't going to lock me up, best I go about the reason I came to town then. Going to place an advertisement in the window of the tourist center and the local paper. I need to start making the ranch pay for itself."

"Thought it already did."

"I get by but having the horse trail rides will be extra cash I'm going to need to help raise my boy. Need the money to add a room to the ranch house too. That's if he gets to stay with me. Kid should have his own room." The thought of not being able to see his son go to sleep on the ranch hit him hard. He'd not thought that far ahead until now.

Rory stood up and came around the desk, placing his hand on Tyson's shoulder. "I'm sure things will work out eventually. Sounds to me like she's still a bit sore over what happened, you not calling her and everything. Women can be a bit temperamental like that. They like the hearts and flowers kind of thing." He grinned and nudged Tyson with his hip. "You might have to do the chocolates and flowers to soften up her bad mood. You know you want to."

Tyson tried to smile but it got stuck in his throat.

He coughed and slid his gaze to his brother. "You mean woo her like in dates and things?"

How on earth would that work? She didn't want him. Layla had made that clear.

"Yeah. Can't hurt to try and patch things up. It might

not turn out the way you want it to but at least you might end up better friends than you are now and it looks like that's all she wants from you. Not coming across like you're enjoying that. Am I right?"

"I guess you are." Now Tyson grinned, the possibilities racing through his mind.

Friends was better than enemies and they were so close to that now it scared him. He had to try and regain some ground with her.

"Reckon it would be worth it. I don't have the money to take her to fancy restaurants or anything. It's all tied up in the ranch."

"What's to stop you taking her on a picnic up the mountain or sending her a bunch of wildflowers?"

Because she doesn't want that kind of relationship, that's why.

"Chance, Pa, and I were talking too, since you mention the extra bedroom. We want to help you add a room to the ranch house." He cleared his throat. "Kind of a good bonding experience for all of us anyway now that Chance and Pa are getting on better and we want to show you how much we have your back, even when some days it might not look like it."

Tyson gaped at his brother. "Seriously? You guys would do that for me?"

"Of course we would. You're family. Why wouldn't we help you?"

Chapter Fifteen

"**W**HAT ON EARTH are you doing here?" Emily put down the phone and hurried from behind her desk when Layla opened the door to her business. "Doctor should have more sense than letting you come back to work after what you've gone through today." She rushed over and took Layla's arm, holding onto her as she led her boss into the office.

Once Layla sat down behind her desk, Emily let go of her and huffed out her breath.

"Don't understand why you came back to work. You should be resting up at home."

"Because I have appointments I have to keep. Days are short enough as it is now you shoo me out of the office early every afternoon, so I don't have a choice." She leaned back in her chair, rested her hands over her stomach and sighed. An afternoon nap sounded like a good idea but she couldn't see that happening any time soon.

"Already canceled your appointments, filtered them through the next couple of weeks so you can pack your purse and head on home." Emily stood with her arms folded and a no-nonsense expression on her face and Layla knew better than to try and argue with her. "Crease and Nate Hansen have both called to try and find out what's going on too. Told them to mind their own business and leave it be. Poor Rupert isn't dead yet and they'll have to wait until he is to find out what's in the will."

"That's one reading of the will I'm not looking forward to." Layla closed her eyes and sighed.

Five minutes to home and her nice comfy bed, she was so there already in her mind but business came first. A flutter startled her and she sat up.

"You okay?" Emily leaned down and looked into Layla's eyes, Emily's hand resting on her shoulder.

"Yes, thanks. Baby moved and I wasn't expecting it." Tears filled her eyes. "It's silly, I know, but I was kind of worried something would happen to him when I got knocked out."

"Understandable and those tears tell me that you really should be lying down. Now, come on, let's get you out of here so you can rest up." Emily reached out a hand to help her up out of her chair.

"I have too much to do right now. Depositions to prepare for court."

Emily tut-tutted. "Do I have to call Chance to come and take you home? I will you know."

"You wouldn't."

"Try me. You might be the boss here, Layla, but you know I promised Chance I'd watch out for you and I will. Now, I say you should be home resting and taking care of yourself. I'll deal with whatever comes up and I don't expect to see you before tomorrow morning. Is that clear?"

Layla's response was to burst into tears. Emily handed her a couple of tissues and waited while the crying jag petered out. "I'm sorry, I don't know what's wrong with me."

"From memory, I'd say that's hormones. I used to cry over the darnedest things when I was pregnant let alone being clobbered by a stupid idiot that doesn't know his own strength. Seems to me having two burly men fighting over her is enough to send even the strongest woman on a little bit of an emotional charge, wouldn't you say?"

"They weren't fighting over me." Layla sniffled and blew her nose before throwing the tissue in the bin.

Emily handed her the box with a grin. "Oh, yes, they were but for different reasons. Those two have been going head-to-head over everything from cookies to school prom dates ever since I can remember. Makes sense that Jethro would have a go at you considering whose baby you're carrying."

Layla made a strangled sound in her throat and grabbed another tissue.

"Yes sir, those two will be at each other from now until you make up your mind about your future, just mark my words."

"No. You're going too far. Jethro is mad because I won't tell him about what's in the will. You know that, Emily."

Her secretary shook her head and gave her a knowing smile. "I know those two. Because Tyson wants you, Jethro will make it his mission to dig himself in between the pair of you even if he only wants information and a little bit of pillow talk about his grandpa. Him going off at you was his version of foreplay – made you stand up and take notice." The older woman laughed. "Darned silly boy. Handsome as he is, he doesn't get it. Flowers make more of an impression than out of control testosterone and a fistfight."

"Are you serious? He'll hit on me because of Tyson?" Layla found it hard to believe but she hadn't lived in Marietta her whole life, so how could she make a judgment?

"Yep, that's the way it usually works with him. Gotta go and ruin whatever he can if he can't have it. Seems to me he'd be better off trying to make a go of things for his grandpa instead of spoiling for a fight all the time but I guess losing their ma so young threw them out. Rupert did his best but he never could rein those three boys in. Spoiled rotten if you ask me and look where that got them." She shook her head. "You know they're distant cousins of the Watson boys?"

"No, I didn't. How come nobody told me that before?"

"Old Jock married Rupert's only son's sweetheart. So in turn, he married the first girl he laid eyes on and that was

Jock's niece. Fat lot of good that did him, marriage didn't last beyond the birth of those three boys. He up and left, and I hear tell he got killed. Rupert took the family in and I guess you know about how they lost her to cancer when she was only young. From memory, the youngest was only about five years old." She leaned on the edge of the desk. "Always been a bit of bad blood between the families but most of the time everyone ignores it. That is except Tyson and Jethro. Seems to be their mission in life to carry on as much as their fathers did when they were young ones."

"Well, I guess that explains a lot then."

"Yes, it does. Let's get you out of here then." She stood up, slid her hand through Layla's arm and helped her out of her chair. "You go on and rest now, I think that's all the excitement you need." She gripped her arm harder when Layla stumbled.

"Sorry, just a bit light-headed. I'll be fine in a minute." Layla lifted a hand to her cheek and closed her eyes.

"I'll take you, leave your car here. I can pick you up in the morning too, on my way."

"Thanks, Emily, I don't know what I'd do without you."

The front door slammed as they walked out of the office. Tyson stood at the door with a bunch of home grown roses in his hands, a bashful look on his face.

"What are you doing here?" Layla stopped and stared at him.

THE TEARS ON her cheeks made him pause. "Why are you crying? Tell me what's wrong. What did Evan say after I left?" He stepped forward ready to grab a hold of her in case she fell down. The paleness of her skin scared him half to death.

"I'm taking her home, Tyson. She's had a big day and it's all too much in her present state." Emily looked at him, her eyebrows raised.

"No. I'll take her." Layla glared at him, fire lighting up in her eyes. "If that's okay, I mean." He held out the roses he'd cut from his father's garden. "I brought you these to try and cheer you up and to say I'm sorry for scaring you."

Layla reached out a hand to touch the petals before taking the roses from him and raising them to her nose. Tyson's stomach dropped when she started sobbing. He looked at Emily for guidance, totally out of his depth with a crying woman.

"It's alright. Just hormones giving her a hard time after what happened this morning. Nothing a good rest and a cup of coffee won't fix, I'm sure. Take her home and settle her down in bed with a hot drink and she'll be fine." She patted Layla's arm and nudged her toward Tyson.

He put his arm around her shoulders, feeling the tremble as she fought back her tears. Having her in his arms brought back memories he'd tried to put away. He sucked in a breath and walked her out to his truck.

"Let's get you home and into bed." *Idiot.* As soon as the words were out of his mouth, he could have kicked himself. "You know what I mean. Let me get you settled so you can rest." He opened the door of the truck and helped her in, passing Layla the seatbelt when she reached for it. He didn't like the way her face had paled even further, her already light complexion and fair hair only adding to the look. He'd get her settled into bed, make sure she was okay and then leave her alone.

The short drive to her place didn't take long and the thought of leaving her alone when she wasn't feeling the best didn't sit well with him even though he knew it would be the wise thing to do. Tyson pulled into the driveway and helped her from the truck, his conscience fighting with his heart.

"Thank you." He kept his hand on her arm as she picked up the roses from the front seat. They walked up the path and when Layla took her keys from her handbag and fumbled for the door latch, he took them them, slid the key home, and opened the front door.

Together they stepped into the cottage Layla had rented. Straight away the differences between them hit Tyson head on. The decorating was feminine and clean, with an aroma of money his home would never have. The fluffy rugs in front of her cream leather couch looked deep and soft to the touch. White on white with pale colors mixed in to give the place a spacious clean feel. So unlike his little ranch house with old furniture and seventies gold-flecked shag carpet. They were polar opposites and it hit home here more than anywhere else.

"I'm not leaving until you're tucked up in bed with a drink and a snack and anything else you need so you don't have to get up until the morning."

She glanced at him and he could see the moment she decided to give in and not fight him.

Her shoulders drooped and she let out a heavy sigh. "Fine. Kitchen's through there. I'll go and get changed if you want to make tea. I've gone off coffee of late, a pregnancy thing." Her eyes closed and for a moment he worried she was going to fall in a heap. Just as he reached, ready to catch her, she opened them she seemed more in control. "There's a fruit cake on the counter in a blue tin. I couldn't eat anything more than that right now." Layla withdrew her arm, passed him the flowers, and walked away, leaving him feeling like a fish out of water in her neat, pretty little home full of furnishings that would never look right in his.

Giving himself a mental shake up, Tyson walked in the direction she'd indicated, placed the roses in the sink and found the kettle. He filled it with water before he convinced himself that looking through her cupboards for a cup and saucer was nothing like going through her lingerie drawer. The delicate gold edge china felt paper thin in his hands and just carrying it from the cupboard to the counter where the kettle blew steam was fraught ridden with nerves for him. He was certain if he held it too tightly, it would shatter.

Tyson took a moment to look past the breakfast nook out the window to the small backyard. Large green trees hung over a small deck where pots of colorful plants brought color to the green landscape. It looked as though Layla had settled in here well. He should be thankful for small mercies. He was happy she was living here and not back in the city so he would at least get to see his son grow up.

But it still wouldn't be enough for him. Would she let him take the boy camping up in the mountains to teach him basic life skills or would she try and bring him up like a city kid, too scared to go and get himself mussed up in the dirt or explore the wilderness like Tyson had been allowed to. Tyson wanted to teach him how to track and hunt too, just as his father had done for him before he found solace in the bottom of a bottle and all of their lives had changed. Dirt never hurt anyone – he was testament to that fact. But would Layla put her foot down where that was concerned?

Just one of the many thoughts that raced through his mind when he couldn't sleep at night, when he lay in the bed they'd made love in, wishing she was there with him so he could hold her while she slept. In his dreams, Layla faced away from him when she slept, her cute butt tucked into his crotch, her hands resting under her cheek on the pillow.

Tyson cupped her breast in one hand and the other had rested on her belly, a belly that now held his child. What he wouldn't do to have that opportunity in real life. To feel the ripple under her skin as their baby stretched its little arms and legs, fumbled in his mother's womb with his hands and grew into the little boy Tyson couldn't wait to meet.

The click of the kettle switching off startled him and he reached for the jar of teabags, grabbed one and dropped it into the cup. He poured the boiling water over it and while it sat brewing – Lyla had shown him that weekend how to make the perfect tea for her – he opened the cake tin and cut her a couple of slices and put them on a matching delicate plate.

A blue tray sat on the counter and he placed the cup and cake plate on it, took a steadying breath and walked out of the kitchen towards the room Layla had gone in when they arrived. He paused outside the door, trying not to peek in the gap in case she wasn't ready for company.

"Okay if I come in?" He waited for her to give the okay.

"Sure, come in."

The bedroom décor didn't surprise him after being in the kitchen and he'd poked his head into the living room, giving it a quick glance over. White on white with a couple of bursts of color to brighten it up. Expensive and nothing like what he was used to.

He stepped over to the huge bed and placed the tray on the cabinet beside it, pushing a book out of the way. Then he stood self-consciously looking around the room before she nodded her chin. Tyson sat on the edge of the bed.

Layla had her head back resting on the overstuffed pillows. Her skin had a see-through tone to it, lines under her eyes competing with the purple shadows. Instead of the woman in charge, she now came across as frail and exhausted and it terrified him. The white nightie she had on did nothing to add color to her face.

"Don't fret, Tyson. I'm okay." She reached out and patted his hand and before he thought about it, he linked his fingers through hers.

Gina had never looked this frail. Nor had Denver. He was convinced there was something wrong with Layla and it left a hollow feeling in his gut.

The more she protested the more he became convinced. "Funny, I don't agree. What happened today was enough to upset anyone and you being pregnant and all..."

"Evan said I was okay. You were there, you heard him." She closed her eyes and he could see her throat working and he wondered if she was fighting tears again.

"Okay, I'll believe you for now. Why not drink your tea while it's hot and then snuggle down and close your eyes?"

"You don't have to stay. I'm in bed and I won't be going anywhere or doing anything. I'm too tired to even think of getting up anyway." Layla gave him a halfhearted smile, one that didn't quite reach her eyes.

"I'll go when you're asleep. Now drink this." He handed her the fine china cup and watched while she sipped it.

"Perfect. Thank you."

"You're welcome. Now, where can I find a vase or whatever you call them for the roses?"

"They're from your father's garden?" When he nodded, she smiled again. "They smell so much nicer than shop brought ones. Make sure you tell him I said thank you."

"You can tell him yourself, said he was coming over tomorrow to mow your lawn. Now, that vase?"

"Sorry. Under the kitchen counter you should find a few."

Tyson stood up, letting go of her hand reluctantly. "Right, drink the rest of that tea and then slide down and close your eyes while I sort out the flowers. I'll get back to the ranch when you fall asleep." He walked out of the room, cursing his overzealous libido.

Even pale and tired, her belly swollen with their child, she was all he wanted. There had to be something he could do to change her mind. Be damned with their differences, he had to have her in his home, in his bed. They could be a team if they both worked at it, Tyson was convinced of it. The battle to convince her was going to be hard fought because there were so many reasons she'd given him why they couldn't be together.

Chapter Sixteen

TYSON SAT ON a chair in the corner of her bedroom, watching Layla sleep. Her mouth open, a hand thrown up above her head, she looked like a snow angel lying amongst the white bedding. He'd made up his mind and even called Rory to talk things over while she slept.

"About time you came to your senses. Hell, if that'd been me, I never would have agreed with what she decided you two needed to do. You gave in too easily, Tyson."

"I know I shouldn't have but you know what Layla's like. A force of nature that many a man would find hard to fight. Probably why she does so well in the courtroom. Anyway, we'll just have to see if we can sort through our problems. I'm not going to let her go that easy." He'd need all the resolve he could muster to stand up to her.

"Have you got over the chip on your shoulder though? Seems to me it was only the other day when you said you weren't good enough for her. What made you change your mind?"

"I still don't think I'm good enough. Not yet but maybe

when the ranch makes more money I'll change my mind. You should see this place, Rory. Looks like it came out of one of those flashy magazines, everything all pretty and perfect. The place screams money. I can't compete with that but I'm going to try."

"I understand that but as a person, there's no one better. Stick to your guns, little brother, and make her see how much you love her. My money's on you."

"Thanks."

"Ah, someone has to bring this up, Tyson. About that ad you placed, what are you going to do about those two women who want to meet you?"

"I don't know. I should have taken it down but I ignored it, kind of hoped it would go away."

"You'd better figure it out before you show your hand then, don't you think?"

"Yeah, I guess so."

He hung up the phone, pushing that particular problem aside, and looked out the back as the sun dipped low in the sky. After all, it wasn't him who placed the ad. Sorting it out should fall to Chance for butting his nose in where it wasn't wanted.

Layla murmured in her sleep. What if she woke up and was hungry? Hadn't Gina always said being pregnant made her ravenous? He didn't want Layla out of bed, at least not until tomorrow when she was feeling better. Perhaps he should think about making her dinner before he left. He hurried out of the bedroom, giving her a final, quick glimpse. She'd pushed down the cover from her body, exposing the small baby bump she clutched possessively. He ached to reach out and touch it, to cradle his son in his hands but he'd only wake her if he tried.

Tyson walked over to the fridge and opened it, taking stock of what was inside. Plenty of fresh vegetables and a plate of chicken fillets covered in cling film. Before he could change his mind, he took what he wanted out and started to create a meal for the mother of his child.

He checked on her every half hour or so and still she slept soundly. Determined to do the proper thing, Tyson decided if he had to stay the night and sleep on the couch, so be it. He didn't want her to wake up alone, not after the day from hell.

There was plenty to keep him occupied in the kitchen cooking on a stove that didn't require a pile of kindling and logs to see him through. He would enjoy making this meal now his mind was made up and he had a future he wasn't going to give up on.

Somehow or other, he would convince Layla they should be together and not purely for the sake of their baby. They had something special and he could see it in Layla's eyes as she lay on the pillows watching him. As much as she denied it, her body hummed when he was around, the same as his did for her.

The only problem was going to be convincing her they

could make it work. It wasn't as though they both got off to a good start. Neither had bothered to make the next move, both convinced it wouldn't be more than a weekend of wild sex. And the mail-order bride debacle had to be cleared up Apparently their son had other ideas and for that Tyson was grateful. Always willing to look for the silver lining, the thought of the baby bringing them together brought a smile to his lips.

LAYLA BRUSHED A hand over her nose and inadvertently touched the swelling on her cheek. "Ouch." Wincing, she pushed aside her blankets, glanced at the clock on her side table and tried to remember why she was in bed so early.

She ran her hand down her stomach and breathed a sigh of relief when she found the small bump of her child. It all came back to her in a rush. The fight between Tyson and Jethro, her getting in the middle of them, and taking a punch to the face for her efforts.

She opened and closed her jaw, working out the stiffness as she prodded her teeth. Everything seemed fine and she remembered Evan had given her the all clear before Emily had all but kicked her out of the office. And into the arms of Tyson. Her heart fluttered. He'd looked out of place and so shy. Then he'd taken over, bossed her around, and brought her home. Ignoring her protests, he'd tucked her into bed with a cup of tea, promising to wait until she fell asleep before he left. And that was the last thing she remembered.

A noise in the kitchen startled her. Wasn't she alone? Layla looked for her mobile phone which she normally kept on her bedside table in case of emergencies. *Damn it, I must have left it in my handbag.* Cautiously, she swung her feet over and placed them on the floor. No head rush. Great. Another noise made her heart patter faster. *Where the heck did I leave my handbag? The closet, of course. I changed into my nighty and dropped it onto the floor.* On tiptoe, Layla hurried to her closet and sighed with relief when she saw her bag.

With shaking fingers, she found her phone and dialed Rory. *Pick up, come on.*

"Deputy Watson."

"Rory, it's Layla. I think there's someone in my house." She whispered as loud as she thought advisable while she sat huddled in the corner of her dressing room, the door closed to a mere crack of light.

"Layla, are you sure it's not Tyson?"

"No. He said he was going home after he put me to bed. I mean, hell, can you come and check for me please? I don't want to go out there in case it's a burglar. I couldn't face another confrontation today."

"I'm on my way. Where are you?" She could hear the sound of keys in his hand and his breathing change as he strode out of his office calling out to the receptionist his plans.

"In the dressing room."

"I'll be right there. Stay on the line, okay, I'm only three minutes away." She heard the truck door slam and the engine kick into life. To keep her mind off her intruder, Layla placed herself in the truck with him and measured every street, every turn until he pulled up at her cottage. "I'm here. Sit tight."

She opened her closet door and peeked out. A shadow passed her bedroom window and headed around the back to her kitchen door. Footsteps landed heavy on the back deck and her heart leapt into her throat. She heard the sound as the door was pulled open and voices reached her. Both of them familiar voices. Hell, Tyson and Rory in her kitchen.

She didn't know whether to be angry Tyson hadn't kept his word and left or happy he'd stayed to keep an eye on her. Layla stood up and reached for her dressing gown, quickly slipping it on before she schooled her features and made her way out to the kitchen where the brothers were arguing.

When she walked in, Rory spied her first and grinned. "Want me to take him in? I have handcuffs."

Tyson turned around and hurried over to her. "I'm sorry, I didn't mean to scare you." He took her hand and looked into her face. "Should you be out of bed?"

She ignored the patter of her heart and the heat of his fingers on hers. "Why are you here, Tyson?"

"How could I leave you when you need me? I didn't want you to wake up and feel alone or hungry so I decided to make you something to eat and make sure you were okay before I headed for home."

"Sorry, Rory. I thought he'd left." Layla withdrew her hand and walked over to the breakfast nook, perching herself on the edge of a seat. "Tell me, Tyson, why are you really still here?"

"I told you. You need me and what kind of guy would leave a woman in your condition alone after what you've gone through today?" He stood watching her, hands on his hips, determination set in his eyes.

She hadn't seen this side of him before and it brought out a sense of… security maybe. But that was beside the point. Tyson was not available, not to her anyway.

"I think this is where I leave you both to it. Try and sort it out once and for all. You're both too damned stubborn for your own good." Rory tipped his hat and left.

"I don't know what to think, Tyson. It's been a hell of a day."

"And I'm sorry for that. I know some of it was my fault." He tilted his head and watched her.

Layla sighed. "No, it wasn't, not really. Jethro is annoyed his grandfather has made changes to his will and I get the whole family connection thing. Emily told me about it."

"Yes, but he wouldn't have given you such a mouthful if I wasn't involved with you. We'll always have history and I heard what he said and for that I'm sorry."

"Tell me, Tyson. What's the real reason you didn't call

me after Rory's wedding and don't say you aren't good enough again? That's wearing kind of thin for me." She shuffled back on the chair and clasped her hands around the baby. "Obviously, you think you're good enough for someone or you wouldn't have written that ad."

Chapter Seventeen

"I DON'T KNOW how many times I have to tell you. Chance took it upon himself to send that to you. I was never going to do anything with it."

"So you say but, the fact of the matter is, you wrote it. In court, I would call that pretty damning evidence."

"You know you'll never believe me no matter what I say, so I don't know why I'd even bother to repeat myself. It's kind of wearing a bit thin, don't you think?"

"Did you do anything with the two resumes I sent to you?" She swallowed and he watched her throat work.

"Really, Layla, do you seriously imagine I would have spent the day looking after you and have a future bride stashed back at the ranch waiting for me? If this is how you think of me, I wonder if we ever had a chance." He ran his hand through his hair and gave her a beseeching look. How the heck was he going to make her understand? "I love you and only you. I knew that the minute that fool hit you in the face. As much as I tried to deny it, there is no one else for me, no one but you. You need to believe that."

"So why did you write the ad?"

"Because I'm an idiot. There's no denying I did it. But at the time I was rotten drunk and it seemed like a good idea to purge it all out. You'd gone back to the city, I was nursing a terrible case of loss and missing you like crazy. It was never meant to go any further than that. Chance should never have stuck his nose in; it wasn't his business."

"Why did you keep it then where anyone could see it?"

"As I said, I was drunk. Hell, you all know how much I disliked it when my brothers did it. Advertising for a wife seems such a last resort kind of thing to do. I don't need to do that, nor will I ever consider a mail-order bride. All I have to do is convince the only woman I love that she is the one."

Layla bit her bottom lip as she considered his words. There were still questions in her eyes and he waited.

"Why did you sleep with me then if it was never going to work?"

"Because I couldn't help myself, that's why." He looked down at his hands and tried to sort out the words in his mind. "I've never met anyone like you. You're strong, independent, beautiful, and know where you're going in life. It's not like you gave me much choice either. You were determined to get me into bed, why would I complain?"

She drilled him with her gaze and he knew this was going to be a no-holds-barred kind of discussion. She had her courtroom attitude on and it showed in spades.

"You have more to offer than you think, Tyson."

Fine, so be it. He wanted to let her know how he felt so this would work in his favor. "Even though I've had time to think things over, I know I'll never have the money you have and that means a lot to me." He held up his hand as she tried to butt in. "Listen to me, then you can have your say." She nodded her head and he continued. "Everything I have goes into the ranch. The verandah leans, the carpet is tragic, the stove requires a cord of wood to keep it going even in the summer." He looked at her top of the range gas cooker with envy. "I have dreams for that place – dreams I can't let go of. They're what kept me going when things got tough, you know, when I was growing up, that one day I'd have my own place."

Tyson rubbed his hand over his chin, felt the stubble rough on his palm. "You were in the city and it wouldn't have been fair of me to call and say, 'Hey, Layla, I want to date you and all but you'll have to give up everything you love to be here with me cause I'm not moving,' now would it? I couldn't leave here, Chance gave me the deposit on my place and I wouldn't do that to him." He laughed, the sound bitter to his own ears.

"Hell, and before I said those words out loud I thought I had a reasonable chance of talking you into a fresh start with me. Hearing them now makes it all sound so feeble, doesn't it?" He sighed and looked at her again. "And your past. It makes me understand why you think the way you do."

She glared at him, the storm rising in her pale blue eyes.

"You are such an egotistical fool. You work hard, have goals and dreams, and don't think that's worth sharing with someone? Is this a normal cowboy attitude or purely a Tyson Watson kind of thing?" Layla wiped a finger under her eyes and sniffled. "Why don't you forget that last comment and my past experience and tell me what you really think, why you thought you had a chance to convince me to stay with you."

Fine, nothing to lose now. He stepped over to where she sat and dropped to his knees in front of her.

Tyson took her hands in his, rubbed his thumb over her knuckles and swallowed. "Layla Cox, I'm a stupid fool and I fell in love with you the moment I met you, only I didn't know it. You made my heart all but stop when I saw you at Chance's place. So damned pretty and self-assured, determined you could get custody of Fisher for the family." He smiled at the memory. "I wondered then what it would be like to have you in my life and do you know the image I had was of you, walking down to the barn holding hands with a blond haired toddler who was calling out to me, eager for my attention. I was a goner right there and then but, as you know, I didn't think I had enough to offer you so I didn't. But you took over, managed me, and took what you wanted." He laughed. "I couldn't stop you, nor did I want to. It was all I clung to, the dream of what we could be, knowing it was wrong of me. I thought that all I had to offer you was my heart, my soul, but not anymore. You already own them."

He rested his cheek against her belly, desperate for contact with his child in case this was the closest he would get before it was born. For all Tyson knew, he'd blown whatever chance he might have had by not leaving when he said he would.

A small hiccup made him look up. Tears streaked down Layla's cheeks.

He reached up and cupped her face in his hands. "What is it? Did I say the wrong thing again?"

She laughed through her tears. "No. This time you got it right. I love you, Tyson. I really do. I can't believe we've been so stupid over this whole thing." She sniffled and tried to swallow her tears. "It's my fault, I know it is, hanging onto my outdated ideas because of one failed relationship. I'm such a control freak; I probably scared you away more than anything."

Layla wrapped her arms around his neck and placed her lips against his. He returned her kiss, hungry for a taste of what he'd been missing. They stayed where they were, both content to hold each other after months of being alone and wondering what their future would hold.

A RUMBLE AND gurgle interrupted the silence. He looked into her eyes.

"Sorry. That's plain rude." Layla laughed and patted her belly as Tyson smiled at her. "I need food. That slice of cake wasn't enough. Being pregnant makes me so hungry."

"Pleased to hear it. I've been slaving over a hot stove while you've been sleeping away the afternoon. I couldn't leave without making sure you were okay anyway so I made you a chicken potpie for dinner." He pushed himself to his feet and grinned at her sheepishly. "Besides you have the best kitchen I've seen for a bit. Sure makes a change from cooking on a woodstove."

"Tyson, about that."

She stood up ready to do battle. Layla pulled herself up to full height and looked into his already stormy eyes and decided that conversation would wait until later. She needed to tread carefully and not throw her money around. He had feelings and her wealth was a big issue for him, she got that. One gentle step at a time.

"Feed me before I pass out with hunger and then we're having an early night. That's if you want to stay with me."

"There's no place I'd rather be and if we have that sorted, I'm not going anywhere. Now, take a seat and let me get your dinner." He nudged her back over to the breakfast nook and reached for a potholder.

"You look kinda sexy playing cook. I could get used to this, Tyson."

He smiled, the skin around his eyes crinkling in a way that had her heart soaring. He was such a handsome man. So much the outdoors and rugged cowboy type that she never thought she'd fall for. Layla loved that life had thrown her such a curveball. Getting out of the city seemed to be doing her the world of good and the thought of settling down with this man made her very happy. A contented glow warmed her heart.

She almost swooned when he pulled the pie out of the oven. The crisp golden topping had been artfully decorated and a tiny vent allowed steam to rise, filling the kitchen with the most delicious aroma. "Who taught you to cook like this?"

He glanced at her, a hint of pink coloring his cheeks. "Milly. She used to help out occasionally when Dad was under the weather." He hung the potholder on the rail of the stove door. "Yet another thing my brothers used to give me grief about but I enjoy it. Some nights, I fall asleep watching the cooking shows on television. Not particularly manly in my opinion but it soothes me. Makes me feel useful."

Tyson reached up and took two plates from the overhead cupboards.

"Nothing unmanly about being a great cook. I'm never going to complain about you fixing me a meal if it smells as good as that does."

He gave her a lopsided grin and dished up a healthy helping of chicken pie before bringing the plates over to the table. When he placed one in front of her, she closed her eyes and sniffed up the scent of chicken, rich gravy, and herbs.

Before he sat down, he took two small side plates from the fridge and placed them on the table.

"Salad? You made me a fresh salad?" She looked at the pretty plate he'd presented to her. Thins slivers of cucumber and carrot rested on a bed of shredded lettuce. Tiny tomatoes had been quartered and sprinkled with parsley and black pepper. Curls of hard cheese scattered over the top and she picked at one and popped it into her mouth. She couldn't have done it any better if she tried.

Tyson shrugged his shoulders. "You need your vitamins. It was use what you had in the fridge or go out and do some shopping. Not my favorite chore so this was the best option."

Layla reached up and drew him down for a kiss. "Cowboy, if this is what you produce, I promise to take over the shopping if you do the cooking. Deal?"

He pursed his lips, thought for a moment and then gave her a resounding kiss. "Deal." He sat opposite her. "Now eat."

Chapter Eighteen

LAYLA YAWNED AND snuggled her head deeper into her pillow. Her body ached in the nicest way and she wriggled her butt into the heat pressed against her. This was how she wanted to wake up every morning. Snug beside the man who held her heart in his hands. After all the angst of the rocky start to their relationship, she didn't want anything to derail them and take away this feeling.

"You know you're asking for trouble doing that, right?" Tyson's sleep filled voice made her smile.

"Did we do the right thing, Tyson?"

"Making love to you will always be the right thing as far as I'm concerned." His hand snaked down from her swollen belly to the spot between her legs already throbbing for him.

"Maybe we should have discussed things more, made sure this is really going to work for us before we resorted to wild sex." They still hadn't talked about money, the one thing she knew would be a deal breaker.

She rolled over and looked at him. His eyes were closed and a small secretive smiled twitched at the edges of his lips.

Layla opened her legs more to give him access to her heat. His fingers slid down and her breath hitched when they entered her.

"I need to know this is real, Tyson. That I can believe in you to be you to not overthink the whole money and status thing between us. I just need someone I can trust and rely on. A good family person like your brothers who put everyone before them for the good of family without dissecting every bill and bank balance. Can you do that for me and our baby?"

"You know I can. Didn't I promise you that last night?"

"I mean it, Tyson. I don't want a cowboy who has his own way out agenda and says things just to make me happy while all the time you're bitter about what I'm bringing to this relationship. Money can wreck things for a marriage, believe me, I've seen it plenty of times." She moaned as his thumb stoked her. "I want stable and normal. I can't go through the ego thing again. I want plain old boring, toe the line, do things the right way and not go off on a tangent kind of normal. You with me on this?"

"We can make this work, beautiful lady. I know we can." He kissed the hollow in her throat, tracing his tongue along her jawline.

Layla was finding it harder and harder to concentrate on what she wanted to say. "Promising to see things through to the end, leaving things half-baked is a pet hate of mine. If I start something, I like to finish it. I'd drive you nuts if you did stuff like that. Perhaps we should list all our faults up front so we both know what we're getting into, because you didn't listen to mine last night."

"Sweetheart, your biggest fault is talking during sex. If I can put up with that, our life should be pretty smooth." He opened his eyes and smiled before covering her mouth with his. "Seems to me a man has to grow up and act like an adult when a child is on the way whether he likes it or not. Me, well I really like the idea of being a father and a husband. Waking up to you every morning is something to look forward to. And I know just the right way to celebrate that."

After a bout of wake up sex, Tyson hurried to the shower. Layla lay back on the pillows, watched him walk away and sighed. To think they'd come so close to not having a relationship. They were both too stubborn and there was one more hurdle she had to overcome before she'd be happy. Layla slid out of bed and padded into the bathroom, leaning on the door jam as she watched him standing in the shower. He looked up and smiled then tilted his head.

"Why do I have the feeling you're plotting something I won't like?"

Layla grinned and walked into the shower to stand under the warm spray with him.

"I'm going to have my say in this because you haven't been listening to me, not really. I have money, lots of it and I intend to use it, albeit wisely." She held up her hand as he opened his mouth. "Last night you promised me you'd act sensibly, like an adult, not going off half-cocked, so please do me the honor of shutting up for a moment while I speak."

When he clamped his lips tight, she smiled. His impulsive nature was pretty cute but not when it was heading in the wrong direction. "If you want me to move in, which is the impression you gave me last night, there are some changes I want to make first. Nothing outrageous, mind you." She paused and watched as he raised one eyebrow. "Well, maybe."

Layla lifted her hand and traced his nipple, smiling when his skin puckered under her touch. "I love the ranch house and I'd never try and get you to move but even you have to admit it needs a bit of loving attention. I'd like to hire the builder who did Gina and Rory's place up. He did an awesome job of it. Not to take away the character or anything, but make it comfortable and easy for us to live there and have plenty of room for the baby." Layla took a step toward him, her fingers lowering to stop the trickle of water that snaked down his chest to his belly button.

"You're busy getting the trail riding business up and going, plowing all of your money into that, I'm busy in town being a lawyer and we have a baby coming. I'm not sure I want to be lighting the fire every time I want a cup of tea. And you enjoyed this kitchen, so why not? We're a team, aren't we?" She took the final step and wrapped her arms around his waist.

He sighed. "I know I'm not going to win with you but I

still don't like the idea of you spending your money on the ranch. Makes me feel like a kept man." His hands cupped her butt holding her against him.

"You put money into the ranch, so why can't I?" She gazed into his eyes. "Tyson, are we going to be a family or not? Because if we are, I have the right to spend my money too."

"I get that but I don't like it." He held her close, his erection prodding against her belly. "I've already got plans to add on a room for the baby."

"I want to go further than that. We need another bathroom and a decent kitchen. If you're worried about what Jethro is saying, don't. He's an ignorant brat with an axe to grind. This is a partnership, Tyson, and partners share things including expenses. Let me do the house up. The rest of the ranch can be your concern but please let me have some fun?"

She lifted a leg and hooked it around his thighs, pushing herself into him. "I want us to be together and the sooner the house is finished, the better. I promise not to change the character of the place."

Tyson groaned and lifted her up, pressing her back into the corner of the shower. "You, woman, are going to be the death of me." He pushed into her heat, his eyes closed.

"Is that a yes then?" She gasped as he filled her.

His answer came out strangled. "Yes."

TYSON COULDN'T BELIEVE he'd given in and agreed to Layla spending her money on the ranch house. He understood why she wanted to do it and agreed it would be better to fix the place up now before the baby came but still. It didn't sit well with him that she was spending money that she'd earned.

She'd made him a breakfast of bacon, eggs, sausages, and coffee before he gave her a lift to work. Layla sent him on his way with a sensuous kiss goodbye and promises of an equally exciting evening. She sauntered into the office with a wave of her fingers and he could see her first client watching them through the blinds.

He climbed in his truck and headed for home, his heart a lot lighter than it had been for months. Staying in town until the renovations were down would set him back a bit with time. He normally started earlier when he lived at home but it was a sacrifice he was prepared to make. After all, it was way more comfortable in Layla's bed than in his own lonely room.

The horses heard him drive up and called out, no doubt anxious for their breakfast. He pottered around the ranch, catching up on his daily jobs while mentally planning the rest of his day.

Tyson heard the truck door slam and walked from the barn where he had been cleaning out stables. Chance headed down his way with Callie's Australian cattle dog, Sherbet, dancing around his feet.

"Morning. To what do I owe this pleasure?" Tyson

leaned down and patted the dog and wondered again why he'd never bothered to get one. Perhaps when the baby was old enough he would look at it.

Chance stood in front of him, a secret smile on his face. "What?"

"Did you sort it out with Layla last night?"

Tyson shook his head. "Might have known. Can't anyone around here keep their damned mouths shut?"

"Not what I asked you little brother. Spill the beans, now."

Tyson gave up trying to be evasive and let out a whoop, fist pumping the air. "Hell, yes. She's going to move in as soon as the place is sorted. In the meantime, I'll be over at her place at night."

"About time. Talk about keep us all waiting, Tyson." Chance grabbed him and slapped him on the back. "Don't think I could have handled it if you didn't man up and make an honest woman of her. The ladies will be pleased."

Tyson snorted. "I thought you were more on her side."

"I love you both dearly but, no, I was rooting for the pair of you."

"So, is that the only reason you came over?" He looked over at his broncos, watched a couple of young horses prancing around the paddock.

The breeding program was finally coming together. With any luck he'd be able to sell off stock before the snow came and invest the money in the ranch.

Chance followed his gaze. "Actually, I had a call from one of my old contacts yesterday. He's looking for some broncos. I told him you had some almost ready for sale. Jake pays well if you're interested. Damn sight more than you've been getting lately anyway."

Interested? That's an understatement. "You know I am. How many is he after?"

Chance took a slip of paper from his top pocket and handed it over. "You call him and sort it out. From my understanding he'll take whatever you have. I have a shipment of bulls going in a couple of weeks so if we can organize it that the broncos get picked up at the same time…"

"Sure. Thanks."

"How did Layla talk you into letting her spend money on the house?" Chance leaned on a fence post and picked a stalk of grass, poking it between his lips as he watched his brother.

"Yeah, that. Got one over me. I tell you, that woman is too damned clever for her own good. Said that we were partners and I agreed, then hit me with 'well you put in money, why can't I? What was I supposed to say to that?" He kicked at the dirt, knowing full well there was nothing he could do about it if he wanted a happy life from now on. Even he'd heard the saying, happy wife – happy life. Besides she was worth it as far as Tyson was concerned.

"She knows her own mind, I'll give you that. Don't forget I warned you ages ago. Seems none of us have a hope in hell of winning an argument with our ladies. They're all much cleverer than we give them credit for. Easier to go along with it if you ask me."

"That's what I was thinking too. I know she's right about putting in some of her money but it doesn't make me feel like I'm in charge."

"You're not. Get used to it." Chance whistled to Sherbet who had wandered off to sniff around the barn. "Are you going to get married?"

"Was thinking of asking her. Kind of like the baby to have my name."

"Why don't you ask Pa for our mother's rings. Nobody else has used them so you may as well. I'm pretty sure he'd like that."

"You wouldn't mind?" He wondered if Layla would mind a bit of family nostalgia.

"Wouldn't have said anything if I did. Layla might be miss modern business woman but I know for a fact she has a soft spot for sentimental things too." He patted Sherbet and then nudged Tyson. "Go and ask her but stop in and see the old man first. He complained not long ago that none of us had thought to use Mom's rings. And I'm pretty sure he'd like to be the one to tell you, 'I told you so.'"

Chapter Nineteen

LAYLA LOOKED UP when her office door opened and Rory stood there, his face pale. She pushed herself to her feet, heart racing. "What's happened? Tell me."

"It's Fisher, he's missing. Gina fell asleep after she put him down for his afternoon nap and when she woke up he was gone. I'm heading up there now with a couple of men. Could you go and see Tyson, get him to meet us at my place. We need all the help we can get and he isn't answering his phone."

"Of course. I'm sure he won't be too far away, Rory. Tell Gina I'll be there as soon as I get him." She watched him race away, anguish and despair clouding his normally happy face. Layla grabbed her handbag and car keys, relaying the problem to Emily as she strode past her desk.

"Cancel anything I have today. Fisher is missing and I have to go and help them. I'll call when we have news." She hurried out to her car and slid behind the seat.

As she pulled on the seat belt, she sent up a small prayer that the little boy would be found quickly. The weather had started to turn cold again, the snow on the mountains getting lower as the seasons began to change.

Her little car flew over the road up to Tyson's ranch, her soon to be home. She parked in front of the house and leaned on the horn hoping to find him that way. When he didn't appear, she climbed out, slammed the door, and hurried down to the barn. There wasn't any sign of him. Frustrated, Layla did a full circle, scanning the paddocks hoping to see him.

In the distance, she noticed a trail of dust coming her way. She ran toward it holding her hand under her belly, waving her other arm in the air willing him to hurry up. It seemed to take him forever to reach her. She was in tears by the time he pulled up beside her. He pulled the horse to a stop and jumped from the saddle, hurrying to gather her into his arms.

"What's wrong? Tell me, Layla. Is it the baby?" He looked down into her face, fear shadowing his eyes.

For a few precious moments she cried in his arms then pulled herself together. Finding Fisher was more important than giving over to her hormonal tears.

She pushed herself back and looked into his eyes. "It's Fisher, he's missing."

"What, no." He looked devastated and glanced over his shoulder toward his brother's property. "Tell me what happened."

Layla relayed what she knew and tried to get him to hurry over to Rory's where he was organizing a search party.

"No. Let me think just a minute. If he wandered off and isn't anywhere near the house, I'd be better going from my side over the hills. Their place leads into mine and Chance's ranch. He'd follow the natural fall of the land, not go climbing hills – he's too little for that. He has to end up in the gully, I know he does." She watched as his mind raced, muttering to himself.

"But, Tyson, Rory wants you over there. He asked me to get you there as soon as I could."

"Go and tell him I'm doing it this way. I'm the best tracker in the family and he knows it. Instinct tells me I'd have a better chance of finding him going in from this side of the hill. Go." He grabbed her and kissed her soundly. "I need to gather supplies in case we don't find him tonight. If he's been missing for more than a couple of hours he could be miles away by now."

"But, Rory said…"

"Trust me on this one. I know what I'm doing."

"You promised me sensible, Tyson." Tears streaked down her cheeks but she couldn't get him to do what his brother requested.

It was as though he'd shut off and was following his own agenda regardless of what others wanted. She'd never felt so out of control as now.

Layla turned and ran to her car. She could at least support Gina while Tyson went off on his own tangent. Had she just made the biggest mistake of her life by getting back with him? She'd asked for stable, boring, fit in with the rest of the family kind of partner, not someone who had their own piper to follow.

TYSON GRABBED BLANKETS, water, and a basic first aid kit as well as a couple of power bars for energy. Layla was disappointed in him for not following her instructions but he was also sure that Rory would back him on this decision. After all, he was the one with the nose of a bloodhound. They teased him about it often enough. There wasn't time for a drive over there and a discussion. Fisher's life was at stake and his brother would understand.

Layla drove off in a cloud of dust, a small part of him wanting to try and explain to her why he was doing what he was but time wasn't on his side. She'd have to trust him on this one. Tyson unsaddled the horse he'd been out on, let it loose in the paddock, and called up his best horse. He threw the saddle over him and cinched it tight. The mare he'd ridden stood in the paddock watching them. He'd thrown her a biscuit of hay and left her without the usual hose down and he could tell she wasn't happy with the deal. His attention went back to the horse he was taking out now. The big animal stamped its feet, the tension from Tyson probably rubbing off on him.

"I know, boy. It's been a long time since we've had to go searching for anyone. Let's hope this time it turns out better for all concerned. I couldn't face another body like last time." He tried to push the memories from his mind but with Fisher out lost, Tyson had to face the fact he might not find the little boy alive.

Tyson had been called in to help search for a missing teen not long before Rory moved back to town. The sheriff had given him strict instructions on where to ride and how long to take. Tyson had argued, insisting a storm was headed their way and he only had hours of clear vision ahead of him. Hours that could have been better put to use with him searching the trails that couldn't be accessed by trucks. Trails he knew better than anyone. But he wasn't the boss and did as he was told – only to regret it the following day when he finally got to follow his instinct and found the body of the young man frozen in a snowdrift.

He wouldn't let that happen to Fisher but it was something he would deal with later, after the boy was safe back in his mother's arms. He could explain everything then and calm Layla's frazzled feathers, if she would listen to him.

Tyson stuck his foot in the stirrup and hauled himself up into the saddle. "Let's go, boy. We have a lost baby to find."

Chapter Twenty

LAYLA HURRIED DOWN the hill toward Marietta and turned left toward Gina and Rory's ranch. They would be beside themselves, she understood that but now she had to add to their angst and tell them Tyson had gone off on his own and wouldn't be joining the search from their side of the ranch.

When she pulled up at the house, she saw Chance's truck, Rory's sheriff's truck, and a few more she didn't recognize. She hurried out of her car and barged through the front door, not bothering to knock. They were all congregated in the kitchen with a map on the table.

"Layla, you came." Gina sat at the table, her face pale and streaked with tears.

"Of course I came. Don't worry, honey, we'll find him, I promise." She wrapped her arms around her distraught friend and fought down the emotions that threatened to choke her.

"Where's Tyson?" Rory pinned her with a gaze that spoke of tense anger born of worry barely held in under the surface.

"Uh, he's gone looking from his side. Said you'd understand and it was a waste of time coming over here to tell you that."

"Typical." The voice was bitter and Layla turned to look at Jethro Hansen. She hadn't noticed him standing with his brothers before. "We all know what happens when Tyson goes off on his own now, don't we? Just ask the parents of Simon West."

"What are you talking about?" Layla gripped Gina's hand, a tremor of cold washing over her body.

"Poor kid was found froz—"

"That's enough." Chance slammed his hand on the kitchen table to get everyone's attention. "We all know why that happened but now is not the time or the place for you to start stirring up old business, Jethro. Fact of the matter is, my brother is one of the best trackers in Montana and we all know it, so if Tyson says he should go in from the back, that's where we should all head to as well." He pointed to the back of the property on the map. "This here is where this ranch meets up with Tyson's. I suspect he's thinking that, because of the way Rory's place veers into a gully, if Fisher has made it further than the first paddock, he'd naturally head in that direction because of the fall of the land."

Rory coughed to clear his throat. "I agree. I think we split up into teams and all head for the back boundary. Pa, you come with me in the truck. Chance, you take Callie on the horses and Jethro, I'd appreciate it if you and your brothers could work as a team together." He held out his phone. "Keep in touch and call if you see anything at all."

He turned to Layla who had her arm around Gina. "If you could stay here and keep an eye on Gina for me?" His voice wobbled dangerously and Layla's stomach clenched at the unshed tears in his eyes.

"Of course I will." She squeezed her friend's hand, noticing the clamminess of her skin. Gina's complexion was paler than Layla had ever seen it before.

He tipped his chin at the back door and Layla excused herself and followed him outside. Rory stood with his hands on his hips and looked at her. "If she looks any worse than she is now, call Evan. I'm hoping this isn't going to put her into early labor but I wouldn't be at all surprised. I think she was feeling a bit out of sorts this morning anyway, probably the reason she slept so long this afternoon. I tried to get her to go in and see him but she refuses to leave until we find Fisher."

"Of course, I'll take good care of her." She swallowed and looked him in the eye. "I'm sorry I couldn't get Tyson to come over. I tried, Rory. Seems he's not one for following the rules."

"I know that and sometimes it gets him into more trouble than it's worth. Not your fault, Layla. Take care of my wife." He called out to the team and hurried to his truck.

Callie squeezed her arm on her way past. "We'll find

him. Don't worry so much."

"I can't help it. I feel responsible somehow." She watched them run down to the barn with Sherbet on their heels where two horses stood tied up and saddled ready to go before she turned back into the kitchen.

TYSON SCANNED THE horizon for anything out of the ordinary. Any small puff of dust or splash of color not fitting the landscape that might give away the cheeky little boy he'd become so fond of. He doubted Fisher would be this far over but a small child could cover a lot of ground in a few hours and well Tyson knew it. He told himself not to think of birds flying overhead. It would be too soon for anything to attract vultures.

While he rode and watched, Tyson had time to think about Layla and their son. She wanted uncomplicated – well so did he. He liked to call a spade a spade and wasn't keen on surprises out of the blue. A steady, calm home life unlike the one he'd had growing up was all he'd dreamed of the nights he lay in bed hugging his ragged teddy bear listening to his father's drunken sobs coming from the kitchen.

The following day, Tyson had hid behind the hedge outside the house listening to Chance trying to talk his father into getting help but that usually ended up in an argument. Despite all of this, he'd been the only son to stay at home when he grew up. To say he felt responsible for his father was wrong, he didn't. He'd lived in hope that something would snap in Pa's mind and he'd get over the anguish their mother's death left behind.

It'd taken a long time but eventually his pa surfaced from his pain and the haze of alcohol to face the world again. Luckily for Pa, Chance forgave him and now they were closer than ever. Tyson swore he'd never put a child of his through the same experience. He wanted to protect and nurture his son, not cry over the loss of his mother whether it was due to a death or a marriage breakdown.

They'd come so close to not having a relationship and Tyson wondered if he'd blown his second chance. Layla hadn't looked impressed when he didn't follow the instructions Rory had given her. Rory would understand but would Layla decide Tyson not complying was akin to going off on a tangent as she so prettily put it? He hoped not. The problem was that they were both so determined to do things their own way and neither of them wanted to be the one that stepped down.

Once Fisher was found, Tyson would try and sort it out but right now this search needed his attention.

He focused on the land ahead and nudged the horse forward. Soon he'd start riding in a grid pattern. He glanced up at the sky, the dark clouds starting to rumble overhead. A fat drop of rain hit him in the face and then another. Within minutes his back was soaked through. It didn't bode well for finding markings to follow. His heart plummeted.

Chapter Twenty-One

"I THINK YOU should lie down for a while, Gina." Layla hovered in front of her friend, noticing the beads of sweat on her forehead.

"No, I'm fine, really." She groaned and held her belly. Bending over.

"Bull. You're in labor, even I can tell that. Why didn't you tell Rory?" Layla placed a hand on Gina's back and rubbed circles as she panted.

"Because he'd make me go to hospital, that's why. I'm not going anywhere until they find my son."

"Can you at least go and lie down then? I'm going to time these pains and see how you go. If I need to call an ambulance, I will and you won't be in a position to fight me on this one. Trust me, Gina, I won't let you stay here and risk these babies." She slid a hand around Gina's waist and helped her to her feet.

Together they walked into the bedroom and Layla got Gina onto the bed.

"I'm going to call Evan anyway once we time these

pains." She slid off Gina's shoes ad tucked her feet under the blankets. "Let me know when you have the next one, okay?"

Tears ran down Gina's cheeks. "I can't believe I fell asleep and lost my little man." She lifted a hand and wiped the moisture from her face. "I thought he was tucked up in bed too."

"He probably was. Look, you're worrying too much and that's not good for you. He may not have gone far at all."

"But it's pouring outside. He's going to get so cold." She gripped Layla's hand. "I'll never forgive myself if they don't find him."

Layla climbed on the bed and turned her back to the pillows so she was comfortable. She needed to take Gina's mind off Fisher going missing and try to keep her calm. "Guess what happened with Tyson?"

"Rory told me you forgave him but he didn't give me the details. I haven't had a chance to talk to you about it." She gave a half smile. "Is it true?"

"Yes. Jethro caused a stir. I'm guessing you know that bit, right?"

"Uh-huh."

"Well, he took me back to my house and put me to bed. It had been a terrible day, what with getting punched in the face from Jethro and all. I must admit, I was feeling rather under the weather." She smiled at the memory of Tyson standing at the door with stolen roses in his hands.

"Emily had decided I was going home for the day and

was pushing me out the door when Tyson walked in. He was so cute standing there with a bunch of roses he'd stolen from Jock's garden."

"That's so sweet." Gina smiled.

"Yes it was. Anyway, he took me home, tucked me into bed with a cup of tea, and then insisted I go to sleep. I thought he was going home but no, the big softy decided to stay and make me dinner. When I woke up I heard a noise in the kitchen." She watched as Gina got wrapped up in the story. "I thought he was a burglar and called Rory to come and save me." How she hadn't put two and two together surprised her. It made sense but at the time she was too stressed to think straight.

"Anyway, we talked and made up. He's being a bit stubborn but I'm allowed to spend some money on the house to make it livable."

"Really? That's so cool. I'm glad you two are getting on, Layla. He's a good guy under all that gruff stuff. He's a proud man, so I suppose you're going to have to accept that and do the best you can." Her face pinched and she closed her eyes.

Layla looked at her watch and made a mental note of the time. Twelve minutes since the last pain. Not as bad as she'd first thought. She'd give it another half an hour and then phone Evan for advice. When Gina dozed off, Layla made the call.

"I'd like you to bring her in but understand that she

won't leave until they find Fisher. It doesn't sound as though she's in labor properly yet though but that could change at any time. I wish I could come up but we're as busy as anything here at the moment." Frustration in Evan's voice made all the more anxious to hear from Tyson or Rory. "Let me know if things change with her and if you hear from anyone about Fisher."

"Of course I will."

TYSON WIPED THE rain from his face. It always made it harder to track when the weather turned foul like this but he wouldn't give up without a fight. He would find Fisher and get him home to his momma where he belonged.

He glanced at the sky. The clouds seemed to be clearing so hopefully the rain would ease as well. With only a couple of hours of daylight left, he had to move fast. If he didn't find the little boy by sunset, it would be hard to continue. He had to think of his horse as well. If it stumbled and broke a leg, they would be useless to Fisher.

Once he crossed over into Rory's ranch his senses went on high alert. Little boys could move fast and they were at least a good few miles from the house. He followed the terrain and pushed his horse toward the gully, keeping a good lookout for anything that would indicate the child had been there.

When the rain finally stopped and the sun did its best to peek out from the clouds, he breathed a sigh of relief. Rain tickled down in rivulets making the way slippery for his horse but Tyson had every confidence they would be fine. He let Rango go down at his own pace while he scanned the area. Nothing moved.

The ride gave him plenty of time to think about his child and how it could be for him and Layla now they had made peace with each other. How close had he come to being a mere visitor in his child's life, having to be content with watching from the sideline and having the occasional visits? The idea left a sour taste in his mouth and he brushed that train of thought away, deciding to think of more pleasant things instead while he scanned the terrain.

A small, muddy shoe floated down a channel worn into the side of the gully. His heart slammed up into his throat. Tyson pulled up his horse and slid to the ground. Beads of sweat broke out on his top lip, his breath hitched in his throat. *No, don't let him be hurt.*

"Fisher, Fisher." He stood holding the soggy little shoe and called until his voice broke. Tears clogged his throat as visions of what could be drifted through his mind. A small child, a gully, and torrential rain that rushed down the sides in their own little rivers didn't bode well for Fisher.

Tyson grabbed the horse's reins and started walking up the side of the gully. He tracked the tiny river of water, hoping that what he would find at the other end would be all he could hope for.

He slid in the mud, lurched forward, and ripped the skin on his palms as he gripped the rocks. Tyson cursed and dug his toes in, started to climb again, a whinny from Rango pulling him up short. He dropped the reins and gave the horse his head, knowing he would find his own way up the rise and wait at the top. Better that than risk his horse falling down like Tyson had just done.

Stones and dirt scattered over his head as Rango launched himself up the bank. Mud squished as it tried to suck down the hooves but the horse was too strong and hell-bent on making it up to the top. The last couple of feet, he struggled wobbling precariously on the lip of the bank. With a final push of brute strength, the horse clambered over the top and found solid ground. He shook his head, the bit rattling on his teeth.

"Good boy. Good boy, Rango." Tyson rested his head on his hand for a moment, letting the relief ease the tension from his muscles before continuing his climb.

He'd jammed the shoe in his jacket pocket, determined on finding its owner alive and well, if not a little wet and bedraggled. He owed his brothers more than he could say and if this was the only thing he could do for them, he would come up trumps. After all, he had a reputation to uphold.

Tyson pulled himself over the edge and lay flat on his stomach, trying to get his breathing under control. Rango, head down, snuffling a tuft of grass, stood a little distance from him.

"Good boy. Here, boy." He held out his hand as the horse walked over to him.

With his hand on the horse's leg, Tyson pulled himself up to a sitting position, then used the big bay to hold on to while he found his feet. Unsteady to start with, he managed to find his balance and heaved a sigh of relief.

The small river still trickled toward the edge of the gully and would probably run for hours yet. With no time to waste, he hoisted himself into the saddle and followed it, praying they would find Fisher before the evening sky became too dark for him to see. As he rode, Tyson called out, hoping for an answer.

He rode for another half an hour that seemed to stretch on forever. With a mere hour of daylight left, he paused for a moment to study the ground around the pool that marked the beginning of the stream he'd been following. The rain had ceased over an hour ago but it still trickled into the depression in the earth to overflow and head down into the gully. Tyson picked up a stick and poked it into the water, testing the depth.

Satisfied the child wasn't in there, he turned and called out. "Fisher. Buddy, where are you?" The only sound that reached his ears was the cry of the eagle soaring up in the clouds above him. He took the reins in his hand, tried not to get too saddened yet and started to walk, looking for footprints, anything to lead him to his nephew.

It took another fifteen minutes before Tyson found any sign of Fisher. One tiny shoe print and a bare footprint beside a small puddle, almost washed away by the rain. "Thank goodness. I was beginning to lose hope in my own skills." He stopped and listened, waiting for a cry to lead him to the boy. By Tysons calculations, they were only about a mile and a half from the ranch house and he should be coming into contact with Rory and the others soon.

A soft hiccupping sob broke the silence.

Chapter Twenty-Two

"GINA, THEY'VE GOT him. Fisher is safe." Layla sat on the edge of the bed and reached for her friend. She still held her phone in her hand, Rory still talking in the back ground.

Gina reached for it, snatched it up, and held it to her ear. "Rory? Is it true, you found my baby?"

Layla tried to control the tears streaming down her cheeks as she watched as Rory reassured Gina her little boy was safe and well but gave up as her friend broke down and sobbed. She reached for Gina, pulled her against her shoulder and together they cried in relief.

"I can't believe it. He's alive." Gina's red-rimmed eyes shone with relief. "Tyson is incredible. I didn't really know how he did that tracking until recently when we were talking about him doing trail rides." She sniffed and reached for a tissue from the bedside table, sat up and blew her nose. Gina gave a wobbly laugh. "I promise I won't make any rude remarks about him ever again."

"No, it wasn't Tyson that found Fisher. It was Rory,

wasn't it?" She bit her lip, feeling a bit traitorous talking about him like this. "I tried to get Tyson to come over here and go with the boys as Rory asked but he went off on his own tangent. Wouldn't listen to me."

"Well, it doesn't matter. All I care about is the fact that he is safe and well." She rested a hand on her stomach. "Thank goodness, things have settled down here as well." Gina lay back on the pillows and took Layla's hand. "I can't thank you enough for staying with me. I was a nervous wreck."

"You know you don't have to thank me. I want you to stay and rest until they get back. I'm going to put the kettle on and make some sandwiches and soup. These guys are going to be cold and wet when they get in."

Gina pushed herself up. "I'm helping."

Layla heaved a sigh. "I don't think that's a good idea. Evan will insist that you stay in bed." She moved out of the way as Gina slid her legs to the ground.

"I'm fine, honestly. I wouldn't put these babies in danger, you have to understand that. But I want to be up and waiting when they bring Fisher in. I need to see him, touch his little face, and squeeze him tight." She stood up, placed a hand on Layla's arm. "Also I need to be here for the men. They've done an excellent job, going out in the cold pouring rain to find my little man. They deserve medals all of them but I hope they'll settle for a mother's thankful hug instead."

By the time they arrived back at the ranch with Fisher,

Gina had paced up and down the driveway with a torch so many times; Layla almost felt dizzy watching her. The emotion welled up in her chest and she ignored the tears streaking down her cheeks, just thankful the little boy was home safe and well.

Callie dismounted and walked over to her. "You alright? You look terrible."

"Well, thanks a lot. Some friend you are." She wiped her hand across her face and watched the happy reunion. "Where is Tyson?"

Callie stamped a foot and looked over at the group of milling men. "Uh, well, he went home."

"Home? Why?"

"Maybe because he lives there. I don't know. Said he'd done what he set out to do and he was leaving, no point in riding all the way over here to turn around and go back again. Didn't see any reason to argue with the man. He's the hero of the moment." She looked up when Chance walked over and slid an arm around her shoulders.

"Let's load the horses in the float and head for home, wife of mine. I need a soak in a hot bath and a comfy bed – preferably with you in both of them."

"On it. Sorry, Layla, gotta go. Hot date by the look of things." She wiggled her fingers and hurried over to her horse.

"What's wrong, Layla?" Chance looked down at her, waiting for an answer and she knew better than to try and lie to him.

"Who found Fisher?"

"Tyson. Who did you think?" He frowned.

"I thought it was Rory, don't really know why."

"What's wrong? You can tell me, you know that. Did Tyson say something to upset you?"

She shook her head. "Other way around. I think I upset him." She relayed the conversation when she'd gone to tell Tyson Fisher was missing, hating how she sounded like the whiny lawyer who got it wrong.

Chance listened, folded his arms and stared down at her. "Well, let me tell you this. Tyson is the best tracker out. If anyone was going to find the boy it was him. Regardless of what we say about him being an old woman and a gossip, there isn't anyone I'd rather have on my side if I got lost than Tyson. If he says he'll go a different way to everyone else, as much as it might seem the wrong thing to you, let him go." He reached out to her when she swallowed back tears.

"You know what your problem is, don't you?"

Layla snorted. "No, but I guess you're going to tell me anyway."

"You're a control freak, Layla. That's fine in the courtroom but not in family life. Believe me, it doesn't work. I've seen it firsthand when I tried to handle my brothers' lives. Hell, you know how that went down; you managed them for me half the time." He wrapped his arms around her shoulders and pulled her close.

"I know this is all different from what you're used to but if you want it to work, you have to have faith in Tyson. He'd never do anything to hurt anyone. You have to believe that and give him credit for knowing what he's doing." He rubbed her back until she pushed away from him.

Mascara would be streaking her cheeks but didn't care. There was something she had to do. Layla hoped to god it wasn't too late.

"You need a partnership where you're both equal. That's the safest way to live with someone else."

"Thanks, Chance."

She turned to walk away when a hand on her arm stopped her. She turned and looked up into Jethro Hansen's eyes.

"Ms. Cox. I have to talk to you if you have a minute." He held his wet hat in one hand and wiped the long hair out of his eyes with the other.

She could see the tiredness on his face and wondered if Tyson was feeling as exhausted. He'd probably be starving and cold.

"Can we do this another time, Jethro? I have somewhere to be." With that, she turned on her heel and hurried back to the house, desperate to talk to Gina again. Layla needed someone else's perspective on this, someone that had been in the same position where one partner had all the money, although reversed. Had it hurt Gina and Rory's relationship? How had they gotten through it?

I need to sort this out in my head before I go and ask Tyson's forgiveness. That's if he'll ever forgive me for doubting him. You are such a bossy fool, Layla Cox. You need to learn to let others take charge before it's too damned late.

Layla walked into the kitchen and started cleaning up the mess, while keeping an eye on Gina and Rory with Fisher. She wanted this, the closeness they had.

Rory looked up and saw her. He walked over and grabbed her arm, leaning in to talk quietly to her. "Listen, I think Gina is in labor but she isn't saying anything. I want to call Evan. Can you stay for a bit, help me with Fisher in case I have to take her in?"

"Sure. Of course I will." Tyson would still be at the ranch tomorrow if that was how long it took to get to him. She would sort out their problems eventually.

TYSON FILLED THE feed bucket for his horse and hoisted it up on the rail in the dry stall. "We did good, boy." He leaned against Rango's neck and breathed in the wet horse smell that never failed to bring him back to earth and his senses. The last couple of days with Layla around had been what his heart screamed for but after her reaction today, when he refused to do as she wanted, his brain started to kick in.

Sure they were good in bed, that was a given. And she was having his child, but did that mean they would be great together or was she only trying to come onto him for convenience and propriety? His line of thinking was heading toward the latter. They were so different in every single way and today's events just reinforced it.

Heaviness weighed in his gut as he imagined the fights and heartache as their marriage started to unravel as he knew it would eventually. No good would come of them even trying when he could imagine the outcome.

The horse snorted and stamped its feet. "Yeah, time for bed for me too." He ran his hand down the forelock, patted the nose, and walked out. His body ached with cold and fatigue. It'd been a long ride back but he had to put his horse first and he had. Chance had offered to give him a lift home but that would have meant two trips with the horse trailer and call him a coward, but Tyson hadn't wanted to confront Layla right now. His mind was too full of conflict and being around her would only waylay his decision.

He trudged down to the cabin, stumbled in a pothole, and cursed. Why the heck would she want to move in here with him when the place was such a dump? He wouldn't if it was the other way around. Bitterness crept up his throat as he tortured himself about how little he had to offer her. The last thing he wanted was Layla spending her money on the ranch only to have their relationship fall down around them. If there was a way to make him feel emasculated, that was the money shot right there.

Tyson pushed open the door and flicked on the light

switch. He glanced into the kitchen, shuddered when he considered lighting the wood stove to make a meal and instead, reached under the kitchen counter for his bottle of whisky. He kicked off his boots and stomped over to his big, old worn armchair and grabbed the remote. As he dropped down into the chair, he clicked the power switch. The television roared to life.

The sound of a car door slamming startled him and he opened his eyes. The muted television glared back at him, a newsreader sharing the day's headlines. He wiped a hand over his face and ran his tongue around his mouth. The empty bottle lay down the side of the chair and he shook his head, regretting it almost immediately. Hammers tapped out a tune on the inside of his skull.

"What the heck—"

The door burst open and Rory stepped into the room, the bright light streaming in behind him.

"Shut the damned door." Tyson growled and closed his eyes.

"Celebrating already? Would have thought you'd wait for me to wet the babies heads." Rory stepped over to the chair and picked up the empty bottle, a huff of disgust his reaction.

"Don't even start, alright?" Tyson swallowed, trying to get rid of the fluffy coating on his tongue. "Wait. You said wet the babies heads?" He lurched forward in his chair and pulled up short, his stomach threatening to embarrass him.

"Yeah, that's right. This morning Gina gave birth to the babies. They're a little on the tiny side but Evan is thrilled with them."

Tyson stood up carefully and turned to his brother. The glow from Rory was almost too much so early in the morning. Tyson grabbed him and gave him a hug, his eyes misting over for what, he didn't know nor did he care to try and understand. "Congratulations, brother."

"Thanks." Rory looked at him, shook his head. "I think you need coffee and a kick in the butt. You look like crap." He headed toward the kitchen and Tyson heard the tap turn on, rumble in protest, then start the slow trickle to fill the kettle. "If I wasn't so damned impressed with your tracking skills yesterday, I'd be the one lifting my boot to kick some sense into you." He walked back into the room and leaned on the door frame.

"How is Fisher?" He wiped a hand over his face and headed to the bathroom to brush his teeth.

"He's great. Evan came and had a look at him, gave him the all-clear but when he saw Gina, well, he got her to the hospital. She's a trooper, I tell you. That woman sweated and struggled through labor like a pro and now we have the two most adorable babies out."

Tyson finished in the bathroom and walked out. "She's a great woman, no doubt about it."

"Yeah, she is." Rory walked back to the kitchen and made coffee for them.

When he lifted a cup in Tyson's direction, he indicated they go outside. Tyson followed him, grabbing his hat and putting it low over his eyes to combat the morning sun as he hit the porch.

"Thanks." He sat down on the step and sipped the bitter brew, letting it seep into his veins and kick start his metabolism.

"I didn't really get a chance to thank you for finding Fisher last night. Things got a little bit emotional, you know?" Rory dropped down beside him, nudged him with his elbow.

"You don't have to, you know that." Tyson took another slug of coffee, glanced down toward the stables, and watched a motely rooster strutting its stuff to impress the few hens that cared.

"I know you don't like praise, Tyson, but you did a terrific job. Fisher could easily have drowned if you didn't find him when you did. Hell, he could have died from exposure." Rory's voice had turned thick with emotion. "Anyway, I couldn't not stop and tell you the news about the twins and say how much Gina and I love you and appreciate the job you did yesterday. She was beside herself with worry. I don't know what she would have done if you weren't there."

Tyson coughed when his chest tightened, thanks to the picture his brother painted. "Couldn't let down my little helper, now, could I?"

"Word of advice, brother."

"Don't bother, Rory. I've made up my mind." He tossed the dregs of coffee on the driveway, small dust clouds spitting up where the drops landed. "I should have stuck to my guns. She deserves better and if it wasn't for the baby, I never would have entertained the idea of marrying her. We're too different."

"That's bull and you know it. Do we really have to go through this again?" Rory snorted his disagreement but Tyson was determined to stick to his guns.

"No, it's not bull. We disagreed last night on how I should have conducted the search when I'm the one who has the experience. She doubted me and my abilities. Didn't trust me to know the right thing to do. I can't live with that kind of attitude. Don't I deserve someone who believes in me?"

"Yeah, you do. When you look at it like that, you might be right although I don't know if it's worth risking a relationship over. Surely you can talk about it."

"I know I'm right. As much as I love her, it's not going to work between us. She and I have very different ways of seeing things. It's a recipe for disaster and I figure that sooner or later, it will be the death of us and any relationship we have. It's better to do things the way she wanted, sharing custody and living separate." He swallowed the pain. "I'm going to tell her today."

"You should think about this, Tyson. It could affect your whole life." Rory rubbed his palms on his jeans. "You know what I think? You two are more alike than you care to admit. Both so damned stubborn and determined. Couple of control freaks, if you ask me."

"I wasn't asking. Besides, I don't agree with you. Layla is a control freak and that's fine in her job, makes her come out on top more often than not and I admire that about her. But you have me wrong. I've never been a control freak. You guys always bossed me around so that's way off base."

Rory laughed. "No, brother. Think about it. Every time we made you do something, what did you say?"

Tyson shrugged his shoulders.

"I'd tell you to go and do something, like now, and you, you would always say something like, 'soon,' or 'later.' See that's you taking control of the situation. You'd do what I said but only on your terms. Control freak, plain and simple."

Chapter Twenty-Three

"IT'S NOT GOING to work. I thought I'd better tell you now, it's only fair." He slapped his hat against his thigh, avoiding looking at her in the eye.

"But, Tyson, we agreed that we could do this. I'm sorry about last night. I didn't mean to try and tell you what to do." Her heart raced and she couldn't stand, her legs had gone weak at his words. She rested her hands on her desk, afraid to move.

"No, you were right in the first instance. We're too different, want different things out of life. I think if we can stay friends and raise our son between us, it'll be better in the long run than having a messy break up." He put his hat on his head and stared at her. "I'm sorry, really I am. Now remember if you ever need anything, you can call me. I'd like to be there for you when he's born too if you can face being in the same room as me." Tyson turned to the door, reached for the handle. "Let me know and I'll be there."

The door closed behind him and Layla sat stunned. The phone on her desk rang but she ignored it, too shocked at what had just happened.

Emily gave her all of five minutes to herself before she walked in. "Well, don't you look a treat? Chance would have a fit if he could see you now. What's that boy gone and done to make you look so pale and pasty like?"

Layla cupped her hands around the small belly and leaned her head back on the chair. "He's dumped me." Tears welled in her eyes and she tried to push them back.

Damned pregnancy had turned her into a weeping female and she hated it. Layla had never been a crier. Angry with herself, she reached for a tissue and wiped her eyes before screwing it up in a damp ball and throwing it at the trash can. When it kissed the top of the bin and fell onto the carpet, she groaned. Couldn't she do anything right?

"Really, dumped you, you say?"

"That is what I said. He's decided he really isn't good enough for me after all and we're over. Seemed that my original idea of sharing custody and being polite to each other is what he wants." She sniffled, determined to get control of the situation and looked her receptionist in the eye. "If that's how it's going to be, then so be it."

Emily crossed her arms over her chest and made a snorting noise. "As if that's going to make you happy. I think I know you better than that already, Layla. You're just trying to protect your heart. You love that boy, even these old eyes can see that."

"Well, it's not going to happen so I have to deal with it."

She brushed her hand over her hair, making sure every strand was in place. "Right, what's next on my calendar for today?"

"You don't have any appointments until after lunch. Why don't you go outside for a breath of fresh air or go down to the chocolate shop and get yourself a treat."

"No. I don't think so. I want to leave early this afternoon so I can go and visit Gina and the babies so I really need to put in the time now." She bit her lip, not wanting to be told to do anything but sit here and sulk on her own.

"You don't have any late appointments anyway, so that was never going to be a problem." Emily took a step closer to the desk and peered down at her. "I know you, Layla, more than you think. If I leave you here, you'll only chew over what might have been and drive yourself insane. You have to learn when to let go and let the boy make his own decisions. You can't control everything as much as you'd like to."

The words hit her hard. Emily was right, she couldn't control what Tyson chose to do with his life. But she could control how she reacted to it. As much as she didn't want to give up on the idea of them being together, she had to show it didn't affect her as much as it did. At least to the outside world. At home she could drop the act and bawl her eyes out if the need arose.

"You're right. There's not much I can do so I may as well carry on as I was going to do in the first place."

"That's my girl. And I think a breath of air outside away from the office might be good for you. Get a hot chocolate and go and sit in the park for half an hour. I don't want to see you back here before one o'clock."

"I might do that. I think a walk in the sun might be just what I need." She gave Emily a wobbly smile and stood up, reached for her handbag and stepped from behind her desk.

"You go on and enjoy yourself for a bit. Come back to work all refreshed and happy."

Refreshed, yes, happy, doubtful but I'll give it a shot for appearances' sake. Layla stepped out into the sunshine and looked up and down the street, desperate for a glimpse of his truck.

Nothing, that didn't surprise her. He'd probably hightailed it out of town to go and hide at his ranch where he wouldn't have to deal with anyone.

Layla headed across the road to the Sage's Chocolate Shop. She'd been tempted more than once to go inside and take a bag of delicious, gooey chocolates home to devour but so far had been restrained, knowing she would probably pay for it after this little boy was born. But today she really didn't care. A big mug of hot chocolate and a bag of dark toffees was on her mind.

The smell enveloped her before she got inside the door. She sucked in a deep breath and smiled.

"Smells terrific, doesn't it?"

Layla looked at the lady behind the counter. A quick glimpse at her name tag revealed Sage, the chocolate shop owner.

"It smells divine. I can feel the weight going on my hips just by standing here.

"Come on in. I'm Sage, and if the grapevine has it right, you must be Layla Cox from across the road at the law office."

Layla stepped over to the counter and held out her hand. After a brief shake, she pointed to a tray of chocolates. "Yep, that's me and, as you can probably tell, I'm going to indulge in your delectable treats. I've tried and failed to stay away from your shop and now I no longer have the energy to try."

Sage laughed, the soft tinkle filling the quiet shop. "I love it when people walk in here for the first time. Now, what can I tempt you with? Feel free to have a taste test of anything you like."

"I'd love a hot chocolate to take out if that's okay. That way if I indulge out in the sunshine, my excuse can be at least I'm getting fresh air."

"True and, really, what's a little chocolate going to do other than make you feel good about yourself?"

Layla lifted a hand to protectively cup her baby bump. "I guess you heard then?"

"Yeah, everyone knows everything in this town." She picked up a pair of tongs and shrugged her shoulders. "I wouldn't change it for the world but some people hate the way things get around." She reached in and picked up a chocolate and handed it out to Layla. "This is one of my newest favorites, a rich chocolate fudge, dipped in dark eighty percent cocoa chocolate. Gives you a double whammy and you look like you could deal with it right now."

Layla took the offering and bit into it, letting the dark chocolate melt on her tongue. She closed her eyes and waited for the taste of fudge. It hit her slowly, almost seductively. The rich, smooth sugary center with the hint of summer berries filled her mouth.

She opened her eyes to see Sage watching her. "Oh, my goodness, that was a surprise. It's perfect."

"Phew, thank goodness. It's a new one and today is the first day I've put it out." She glanced away then back at Layla. "Listen, for what it's worth and I don't want you to think I'm butting into your business, Tyson is a great guy. I hope you two can work it out."

Footsteps sounded at the door and Sage looked startled. "I don't want any trouble in here, Jethro. I mean it, I'll call Rory to drag you out if you start anything."

Layla turned around, saw Jethro standing in the door-way.

"I'm not here to cause any trouble. I was wanting to talk to Ms. Cox."

"Make an appointment with Emily, Jethro. That's how I do business." She turned back to Sage. "Can I have a half a dozen of those please, Sage and a hot chocolate to take out?"

"Sure."

"Make that two, please, Sage." He stepped over to stand beside Layla. "I won't cause any trouble, I promise, but I would like the opportunity to talk to you for ten minutes outside if that's possible. I'll even pay for the hot chocolate."

"Jethro, it would be best if you made an appointment."

"I'm not going to make an appointment and pay you to apologize to you. Don't seem fair in my book. Just give me ten minutes before you walk back to work, that's all I'll need."

"I'm not going back to the office, Jethro. I'm going to give myself half an hour of peace and quiet in the park with my drink."

"Please, Ms. Cox. Let me walk you there then? I promise not to take up too much of your time."

Sage hovered at the counter, having already bagged up the chocolates. "Still want the two hot chocolates, Ms. Cox."

"Call me Layla, and yes, please." She turned to look at Jethro. "Ten minutes and if you even think of causing trouble between me and Mr. Watson, so help me, Jethro, it will be the last time we talk outside of a courtroom."

"Yes, ma'am." He hovered by the door, a wary look on his face.

She waited for Sage to make the takeaway drinks and to amuse herself and stop her mind from wandering, Layla tried to memorize each different chocolate for future reference. She would be kidding herself if she didn't think she would be back in here now she'd had a taste of Sage's creations.

"Here you go."

Layla handed over the money and took both drinks. She

handed one to Jethro as she passed him. "Follow me, your time starts now."

He scurried down the street after her as she turned left and headed to the little church Rory and Gina got married at, rather than the park in the opposite direction. The quiet of the small rose garden where they'd had photos taken seemed the place she'd gravitate to, to try and gather her scattered wits. By the time she slowed her pace, the old wooden park bench with the rambling, pink rose bush was in sight. Her feet sighed with relief as she sank down onto it. Layla took a sip of her drink and then looked at Jethro.

"Five minutes gone. Better talk fast, Jethro."

"I'm sorry, okay."

"Is that it?" She stared at him, confused. He could have said this earlier and saved them both the uncomfortable silence getting here.

"No. No, it's not. Look, I know you won't tell me what's in Grandpa's will and I respect that." She raised an eyebrow and he sighed. "I do. I've been an ass, I get that. Let him down more times than I can even begin to imagine." He held the takeaway cup in his hands and looked down at his feet, scuffing the grass with the tip of his cowboy boots.

"And you're telling me what I already know, why?"

"Don't know who else I could be talking to. He trusts you so I guess I should too."

"Is there a point to this conversation, Jethro? 'Cause all I'm hearing is you've been an idiot, which we both know, and that's it. Where do I fit in?"

He turned his gaze toward her and Layla saw the pain in his pale blue eyes. "I have to try and make it right before he dies but I don't know how. I figured apologizing to you might be the first step." He took a sip of the drink and pulled a face before putting it down on the edge of the seat beside her. "You know I didn't mean to hit you. I was aiming for Tyson. Not my fault the damned fool moved."

"Okay, so you've apologized. Is that it?"

"No. Not it's not. Not sure if you know the history but Grandpa took us in when our father took off, leaving Mom with the three of us boys. Poor thing didn't stand a chance with trying to keep us in line. Didn't know it at the time but she was poorly and never got better. Died not long after we moved here." He looked at the church. "I remember this place. I can recall her coffin sitting in the front of the pulpit with the good reverend saying nice things about her. Strange because I was more interested in annoying my brothers than anything. Don't think any of us really understood what was going on."

He turned and leaned on the post and rail fence. "Anyway, thing is, none of us have given Grandpa the respect he deserves and for that I'm sorry. I want to make it up to him but I don't know how. I was kind of hoping you would help me out here, considering you're probably going to be the executor of the will anyways. That much he told us but nothing else."

"Why now, Jethro? Why wait until it's almost too late?" Layla started to feel for him and his brothers.

Losing their mother and father so young was bound to have made an impression on the boys and she was sorry it had taken him so long to appreciate the love his grandfather had given them over the years.

"Because I'm an idiot, I guess. So busy blaming everyone for my troubles, I never stopped and thought I could do something about it, take responsibility for my own actions. I blamed Tyson as you know and look where that got me."

"I can understand you holding a grudge, Jethro, but I do think you've overdone it."

Jethro turned and looked at her, leaned back on the rail. "You and Tyson. Are you… together?"

Her skin prickled and Layla remembered what Emily had said about Jethro always trying to push in on anything Tyson wanted including woman. "That's not your concern and I refuse to discuss my life with you."

"He's a good guy, even if I do give him crap. But back to Grandpa. Do you think I have time to make things right with him? He won't talk to be about his health so I have no idea how long he has or what's wrong with him." She noticed a sheen of emotion in his eyes. "I don't want him to die thinking we don't care, because we do. We just chose a lousy way of showing it."

Layla put down her drink and pushed herself up from the bench. She knew Rupert didn't have long and Jethro seemed legit enough. Could she tell him what to do without putting client confidentiality at risk?

"Jethro"—she reached out a hand to touch his arm—"if it was me, I'd do everything I can to sort this out with him now. Don't leave it any longer. Go home, tell him what you told me and ask for forgiveness before it's too late. Maybe you and Rupert can work it out. That's something for the two of you."

"Now? He's really that ill?" The pain in his eyes made her tear up.

"Just go, Jethro. Please make him happy."

He grabbed her into a bear hug and held her tight. Small hiccups and a tremble of his shoulders told her what she already knew, he was full of emotion. Layla was glad for the chance to help him, even if it meant she might have broached privacy rules. This family needed to heal and if she could help, so be it.

She rested her head against his shoulder as he took comfort. The rumble of an old truck as it slowed down broke the moment and Layla looked over the rose bush to the road.

TYSON GLARED OUT the window at the spectacle Jethro and Layla made. So much for her loving him. He had been right to reject her. It hadn't taken long for her to seek comfort in the first pair of arms that reached out. He might have known that Jethro would come around sniffing at her door. A leopard didn't change its spots.

He floored the gas and took off, headed for the only place he felt comfortable at. The ranch. He'd put up posters in all the shop windows in town he could think of that would advertise for him and stocked up on horse feed before heading home after his chat with Layla. Still conflicted over what he'd said, his mind warred with his heart. The only way to clear his head was a ride up the mountains on his horse.

Jethro! That slimy, no-good, godforsaken scum bag! And Layla, not fighting him off or anything remotely like it. How was that possible when not that long ago, he punched her out in the street? Women, he'd never understand them. It might have been better if he'd gone ahead with those replies he'd gotten from the ad for a mail-order bride. Shame he'd thrown them in the fire in a fit of anger.

When he rode back down the mountain later that day, the lights were on in his house. Chance's truck sat outside the door and he groaned. He didn't need his big brother butting his nose in any more today than he did yesterday or the day before.

He took his time unsaddling Rango and settling him down for the night. By the time he got back to the house, all he wanted was to crawl into bed and hide from today's events. The image of Layla and Jethro still burned the back of his brain.

"Where the heck have you been?" Chance looked up at

him from Tyson's favorite chair in front of the television.

Tyson walked in and threw his hat onto the coatrack in the corner of the tiny living room. "Why? What's it got to do with you?"

"Well, since you don't answer your damned phone and those horses need to be ready to go tomorrow instead of the following day, I had no choice but to come and see you. Much as I'd prefer to be at home with my wife, and all."

Tyson groaned. He'd forgotten they'd arranged for them to leave this week. "Sorry. Forgot totally. My mind was on other things."

Chance stood up. "Here's the thing, little brother, business is business and it won't wait while you have woman problems, okay? You make a deal with someone, they expect it to be dealt with and honored. Make sure they're ready by eleven a.m. tomorrow, because that's what time the truck is leaving my place."

"Sure and I'm sorry."

Chance's face softened. "What's going on? I thought you guys had it sorted out."

Tyson walked over and sat down on the old chair at the small dining table. "I thought so too but after the way she carried on over the whole Fisher rescue, I thought about it some more and we really don't have enough in common to make it work. It's only a matter of time before we would break up anyway. I can't go through that, especially not with a child in the mix. Wouldn't be fair."

"Your call of course, but…

"And I saw her in Jethro's arms not an hour after I told her too."

"What, are you kidding me?" Chance jammed his hands on his hips and stared at him. "That doesn't sound like the Layla I know."

"Nope, me either but I wonder how much we really know someone. They were in the church yard, hugging like their lives depended on it." Tyson scraped a fingernail over a scratch in the table. "I should have gone with one of those mail-order brides. No expectations or anything. Pretty sure it would have worked out better, considering."

"Why don't you then? I mean, if you're sure it won't work out between you two and you want a wife, it's not a bad way to go about it."

"Threw them in the fire."

Chapter Twenty-Four

"CHANCE, TO WHAT do I owe the pleasure?" He walked in and stepped over to kiss her cheek before sitting in the chair in front of her desk.

"In town to pick up some gear, thought I'd drop in and see how you're going." He sat back in the chair with an ease in his surroundings that she envied.

"As you can see, I'm fine." She lowered her lashes, lest he see the pain in her eyes.

"Don't lie to me, Layla. You know I can see through you." He shook his head when she gave him a quick glance. "Black marks under your eyes that your makeup doesn't cover. Looks like you went a round with a bad dream last night too."

"Tell me what I want to hear, why don't you. You seem to have lost your charm."

"Tyson burned the replies you got for the mail-order brides. When I spoke to him last night, he made a comment about wanting to hookup and see how it went."

The air sucked out of her lungs and Layla saw stars before her eyes. The sick sensation in her stomach made her ears ring.

"Shit." Chance bolted out of his chair and was at her side in a second. "Sorry, I didn't think it would hit you that hard." He held her by the shoulders so she didn't pass out and hit herself on the desk.

Layla steadied her breathing and brushed his hands away. "I'm okay." She couldn't keep the tears from her voice.

"Bull crap. You're not." He sat on her desk, looking down at her. "Tell me the truth, Layla, and don't try to cover it up. Do you want Tyson?"

She swallowed, the pain in her chest almost too much to bear. "Yes."

"So tell me this then, what was the deal with you and Jethro in the churchyard yesterday?"

"Why?"

When he didn't answer, she sighed and reached past him for a tissue, dabbing at her eyes. "He wanted to talk about Rupert."

"Care to share?"

"Sure, but it stays in this room." When he nodded his head, she continued. "He apologized for hitting me and told me about how hard he's been on his grandpa. Asked me what to do to try and fix things before Rupert passes on."

"Guess better late than never."

"I know he means it, Chance. Poor boy was so upset. I was consoling him when Tyson drove past. If he thinks I'm that flighty, he needs his head examined."

"Sounds to me like you both could do with a kick in the pants. Both too damned stubborn to see what's in front of your face, if you ask me."

"I think it's too late."

"Is Tyson dead?"

"What?"

Chance poked a finger into her hand. "Are you still breathing?"

"What's with the stupid questions?" Layla pushed her chair back and stood up.

"Think about it. He's not married, not dead or dying that we know of. Why is it too late?"

"Because he told me it was."

"And since when have you done what anyone else wanted, Layla Cox?"

She walked to the window and looked out between the blinds, keeping her tongue still.

"You need to step back, Layla, and let someone else be in charge for a change, especially when it's a job they know better than you." She spun around to glare at him.

Chance gave her a smile. He was doing his best to not offend her, but sometimes she needed the words of a friend to bring her down to earth. He made sense and she knew it.

"Do you think he'll forgive me for lashing out at him?" The way she'd laid into him when he went to find Fisher embarrassed her.

She could try and say it was out of fear but deep down

she knew it was because he hadn't done what she'd told him. Layla wanted to be in charge of everything, always had. It served her well in the courtroom when doing battle but in her personal life it didn't go down quite so well.

"I have no idea. Tyson feels things deeply, more so than the rest of us. Probably the reason he stuck by Pa when the rest of us hightailed it out of there. He's the reliable one in the family, always was." He scraped a hand over his chin. "Thing is, we never gave him enough credit for what he did, standing by Pa and putting him on the right track. He not only took the brunt of our jokes as a kid, but the garbage we left behind. Tyson deserves better and I think it starts with you."

"You hit hard, cowboy." The heat raced up her cheeks.

"Learned from the best. You need to know when to let go and sit on the sidelines. It's what makes a marriage work, sharing the load. Might take you a while to learn that but I'm sure you'll do just fine." He reached over and patted her shoulder. "Got nothing to lose, Layla, by admitting you can't be the boss of the world."

"Call it a professional quirk, risk, downfall, consequence, whatever. I'd be toast if I walked into the courtroom any other way." She sighed and rubbed her hand over her growing mound.

"This isn't a courtroom. It's your future we're talking about, Layla. You have to treat it with respect and care." Chance looked at her, his clear blue eyes troubled.

"Spit it out, Chance."

"Fine, you asked for it. How come none of your other relationships ever came to anything?"

"Because they weren't the men I thought they were, that's why." She blushed, remembering Samar and his family's opinion of her.

Layla turned away from him, knowing the words she spoke were a lie. Every single man she'd dated over the last few years had started off fine, then backed away from her. She swallowed as the truth hit home. She'd scared them away and was doing exactly the same thing with Tyson. Only difference here was that there was a baby involved. *You idiot, Layla.*

"Nothing in life is set in stone. Why don't you go over and see if you can fix it? Give him a chance to prove that he's the man you thought he was and let him have a say without you putting the words in his mouth. Or, if you aren't prepared to fight as much as the Layla I know would, print him out another copy of those applications for brides and send him those instead."

Layla owed it to this baby and Tyson to give it one more shot and if it meant she had to grovel and beg forgiveness, so be it. After all, she had been the one to make the most mistakes in this relationship, and that was being perfectly blunt with herself. "You can be so damned hardheaded, you know."

"Back at you. Now I really must get home or my bride will be wondering where I am."

Chapter Twenty-Five

"**M**S. COX HAS approved this one for you as a parting gift. Thinks it's the best offer you've had so far. Don't go messing up, Tyson, or mark my words, someone else will worm their way in there."

Emily thrust a sheath of papers at him, waving them in his face. So, Chance must have told Layla he'd burned the last copies she'd sent over. He'd only said anything about it in a fit of temper. Sore at himself because he'd dumped her, sore because she was the best thing he could have hoped for and, more than anything, regretting he probably wouldn't be there at the birth of his son with the only woman he could imagine spending the rest of his life with.

"Thanks." He took them and dropped them on the closest hay bale. "Don't let me hold you up."

"You're not." She turned and looked up at Copper Mountain, the sun setting in the sky leaving a hazy glow over the snow-topped peaks. "Sure is pretty out here. Why anyone would want to live in the town is sure a mystery to me."

"But you live in town." He frowned and unhooked the girth strap on the horse.

"Only because Mr. Forsythe brought us a house there." She smiled wistfully. "Such a sweet man he was. Bought it before he proposed to me, he did. Thought it was his job to make sure he could provide for me before he made his intentions clear."

"Wise man, I would have said." Tyson pulled the saddle off the horse and plopped it down on the rail.

"Silly old fool is what I told him. If he'd been a little bit less stubborn, we would have been married years before then. But, no, he had it in his mind that a man had all the financial responsibilities before he popped the question. Course, once I said yes and we managed to nut out the yours verses mine problems, things looked up for us. Fifty-three good years together we had before he passed on."

"That's nice." Tyson picked up the hose and turned it on, running it over the horses back.

"Nice, yes, I suppose so. Didn't mean we didn't have our disagreements. Every marriage has that. It's how you deal with them that makes the difference." She reached up and patted the horse's soft white muzzle. "Gotta remember to listen and be ready to accept an apology too. One of the most important things, in my mind."

A niggle of self-doubt itched in his belly. Was there an underlying message here he wasn't getting?

"Best I be off and leave you to it. Don't go ignoring

those papers too long now, Tyson. Hate for you to miss out on a good life." She turned and walked back to her car, taking the time to stop and look at the mountain once more before getting in and driving away.

"Foolish old woman. What does she know about my life?" He turned off the hose and scraped down the horse, drying most of the water from its back before throwing a rug over it and leading it into the stables. Once all the animals were fed, he started to walk up to the house, his stomach rumbling with hunger then remembered the papers Emily had delivered. He went back and grabbed them, stormed up to the house.

After Tyson had toed off his boots and hung up his hat, he threw the papers on the table, annoyed Chance had once again stepped into his business. Yes, he wanted a wife but not one of the women that had answered the ad. He'd only said it in passing, hoping his brother would drop the subject. The only woman he wanted, he couldn't have.

He flicked on the television, turned up the news, and padded into the kitchen to fry up a steak and some potatoes he had left over from the last meal he'd cooked himself. His supply of fresh vegetables was dangerously low and he cursed himself for not getting any yesterday. Pity that Jethro had soured his stomach and made him forget to stop at the grocery store on his way home.

He grabbed the wilted broccoli, last skinny carrot and the large steak from Chance's own beef before he lit the fire in the woodstove. The memory of Layla's newfangled gas cooker poked him in the ribs as the first match refused to catch the kindling.

"Darn fool thing." He struck another match and held his breath while it caught.

Once it roared to life, he shut the door and found a pan. Tyson seasoned his steak, left it to rest on the plate while the pan heated. He peeled his vegetables, put them in a small steamer and left it on the edge of the stove to cook slowly.

By the time he sat down to his solitary meal, his mood was morose and anger only just simmered under the surface. Had he made the biggest blunder of his life? Only time would tell. If he could have a halfway decent relationship with Layla and be there for his child, their short-lived fling wouldn't have been a total write-off.

The papers taunted him across the table. He reached for them, scanned the first page. It was a letter from Layla, explaining the reasons for only giving him one of the applications. She'd decided, upon review, that one applicant was more appropriate than the other. But there was more.

"About you seeing me and Jethro together – I know it's none of your concern but I want to tell you anyway. We were discussing his grandpa and he'd broken down and was crying on my shoulder, nothing more. He is doing his best to make things right between himself and Rupert before Rupert passes on and for that I give him credit."

Rupert passing on?

"Please keep it to yourself but Rupert has only a short time left and Jethro is doing what he can to mend the fences between them. Hopefully they will succeed. There is nothing worse than losing a close family member on bad terms."

So she didn't want to be with Jethro. That made him feel better but he still didn't trust the guy any further than he could throw him. And it didn't change things between them. Tyson flicked over the page and looked at the resume.

It was typed on a page without a header and he started to read. He skimmed most of the information on the page until he came to the 'goals' section.

Goals – My biggest goal is to try and sit back, not let my mouth run off and take over. In my career as a lawyer, I've always been the one to lead the charge, so to speak. I know it's time for me to let others lead, especially where they know more than I do.

Dreams – I dream of having a family. The child I carry now needs his father but not as much as I need the man I love. I hope he can forgive me for being so pigheaded, stupid, and arrogant to say nothing of doubtful. I've always charged forth and taken what I wanted, regardless of what it was, because that is my nature. I need to learn to not be so controlling and to stand back, letting my husband have an equal say in our lives. I'm ready to do that and this is why I feel I will be the best candidate for the mail-order bride.

His heart started to race and he turned the page. *What makes your heart sing? Lying in bed watching my favorite cowboy sleep, the stubble of his beard rough on my palm when I can't resist reaching out to him.*

What scares you the most? Commitment. Without a doubt it

would be this because I have never had to, nor have I wanted to, commit to anyone since my only serious relationship. I was hurt beyond belief but that shouldn't stop me from believing there is someone out there for me. Now I feel that I want this more than anything else but still it scares me. With the man I love beside me, I know I can do it.

What can you bring to this marriage? Regret. Sounds strange, doesn't it, but I regret it ever got to this stage where I would have to apply to get back the trust and love of the man who holds my heart. I admit that it was my fault he left me. I'm a control freak, plain and simple. I'm stubborn. But I'm prepared to try and if it doesn't work out, I won't regret that I gave it my all.

He flicked over to the last page and sucked in a breath. A black and white photo of his son stared back at him and below it, a color photo of the woman he loved, cupping the swell of her belly. A serene smile touched her lips but he could see the tinge of sadness too.

Had he judged her wrong? Could he contemplate making the biggest leap of his life with her?

A knock on the door startled him. He turned over the pages and strode over, ripping the door open expecting to see Layla standing there.

"Hey, man." Jethro Hansen lifted a hand and before Tyson could help himself, he took a swing at Jethro, connecting with his jaw.

"Shit." Jethro fell to the floor, landing on his butt. "Ain't no need for that."

"Get up and I'll do it again." Tyson's mood was dark. Partly because of the application Layla had sent him and partly because of the man sitting on his butt on the porch. "What are you doing here?"

"Can I get up?" Jethro wiped the smear of blood from his lip.

"No. Say your piece and get out." Tyson stood staring down at him, tempted to slam the door in his face.

"I'm sorry. For everything."

"And, what am I supposed to take from that?"

Jethro shuffled back and got to his feet, his arms out to keep Tyson away from him. "I told Grandpa I had to come and apologize to you. For all the shit I've given you over the years, the pain I've caused him doing it. Wasn't your fault your father and mine fought over a woman."

"And what does that have to do with Ms. Cox?"

"Sorry if you got the wrong impression yesterday. I asked her advice about how to go and fix things. I know she wasn't going to tell me nothing confidential but we talked and, well, I'm not ashamed to say I cried on her shoulder, some." He wiped a hand over his face, his eyes misting over. "Didn't mean to but it was what it was. See, the thing is, Grandpa is sick and he's asked her to take over and sort out his affairs before he goes." Jethro sniffled and lifted his chin. "Been pains in the ass for more years than I can count but I'm trying to fix things between us if I can."

"Uh-huh." Tyson leaned on the door frame, content to

keep his fists to himself for now.

"Well, I know how she loves you and the baby and stuff. I wanted to make sure I didn't cause you two any trouble, like come between you or anything."

"Nothing can come between us, certainly not the likes of you." The words hit him in the face as soon as he said them out loud.

Hell, he was a stupid fool. He'd let so many things come between them. His stubborn pride, her career and money. His living arrangements and lack of ready cash.

"Anyway, I had to apologize. I'm sorry for all the nasty things I said and all the times I got in your face. I hope you can forgive me." He held out his hand.

Tyson raised his head, looked the man in the eye, and knew he meant it. Tyson reached out, took the hand offered and gave it a quick shake.

"Thanks. Good luck with Ms. Cox, too. You're one lucky man, having someone like her to love you. I hope I get as lucky one day."

"I doubt she loves me after what I've done to her. But thanks for the apologies anyway. I appreciate it." He watched Jethro walk toward his truck.

He turned as he reached for the door handle. "She's pining for you. Any fool can see that. Better go and claim her before someone else does." With that last parting word of advice, he got into his truck and drove away, leaving Tyson standing staring after him.

Chapter Twenty-Six

THE BANGING ON the door woke Layla from a troubled sleep. She sat up on the couch where she'd nodded off watching television, pushed her hair back from her face, and wiped at the tears she'd cried. The hammering sounded on the door again.

"Layla, are you alright? Open up."

Tyson? Here?

"Layla?"

She stumbled to the door, tying her dressing gown as she went, trying to cover the baby bump that kept making the garment slip to one side. She opened the door and stepped back. Tyson loomed in the doorway, his hair mussed up, his cheeks flushed.

"What's going on? Why are you here?"

"Because I have to apologize, that's why. I… look, I didn't mean to hurt you yesterday. I just thought it would be better if we stuck to the previous arrangements. Less chance of us fighting and breaking up eventually."

"I get that so why are you here then? Ready to rub more

salt into the wounds?" She turned and walked away. Yesterday, she'd been so keen to go and see him after her talk with Chance but common sense had won out and she'd driven herself home instead. Today, the idea had crossed her mind again but she'd talked herself out of it, not wanting to put her remaining threads of self-preservation and respect on the line and risk getting hurt all over again.

"No. I want to take you up on your offer. If you still mean it, that is?"

Layla turned to him, wrapping the gown around her belly and holding it there. Tyson's gaze went to her hands and she saw the conflict in his eyes.

"What offer? I don't understand, Tyson. Probably because you woke me up but maybe you'd better fill me in here. I swear I have baby brain these days." She curled her foot up under her butt and snuggled down on the couch.

He closed the door and followed her into the lounge. "You answered my ad for a mail-order bride." He licked his bottom lip and watched her.

Oh no! "I… I did?" *How the heck did that happen? Emily, Chance, I'm going to kill the pair of them!*

"Didn't you?" Color washed up his cheeks and he started to back away.

She hurried to her feet, stumbled, and fell against the coffee table, thumping her knee and crying out.

He lurched forward, grabbed her, and pulled her into his arms. "Are you alright?" He ran his hands up her arms, over her hair, and cupped her chin in his hands.

The look of sheer panic on his face warmed her heart. He did care for her, that much was obvious.

Layla rubbed at her knee, cursing her stupidity. "Shaken but fine. Listen, Tyson. Sit down and we can talk, okay?" She returned to the couch and patted the cushion beside her.

After a moment, he stepped over and sat, keeping a distance between them.

"So, tell me about this application I sent you. How did you get it?" She hadn't even printed it out when she filled it in, in a fit of jealousy.

"You sent it with Emily. Didn't you?" Realization slowly dawned on his face and a slow "oh" came from between his lips.

"Yes, oh." She smiled, albeit a little tearfully and reached for his hand. She took it, wound her fingers through his. "We are such lame ducks, Tyson. I think I just got paid back for looking for a bride for you."

"So you didn't apply for the job then?"

She watched the light fade in his eyes and hurried to put it back. "Yes, I did but I didn't ask Emily to bring it out. I did it in a fit of temper but didn't have the nerve to go that far. Not yet anyway."

"So you're taking it back then?"

She pondered the question. "No, I'm not. It's out there now and I meant every word I said. I didn't want to embarrass you by sending it but I would have plucked up the courage sooner or later, I know I would have. I want you, Tyson, I always have. I just didn't go the right way about telling you and for that I'm sorry. I let my compulsive, controlling personality get the better of me and it's time for me to change that."

"You'd do that for me?" He slid closer, held her hand a little tighter.

"Yes. I'd do anything for you. I want you to know that."

"Move into my rundown old ranch house and live with me like it is?"

She held her breath. "Yes, even that, so long as we're together, the rest doesn't matter."

Tyson smiled and pulled her into his arms. "I wouldn't be so mean as to make you cook on that old stove. Even I hate it after using your gas wonder. Layla Cox, would you do me the honor of becoming my wife?"

She rested her cheek against his. "Tyson, I need you to be sure this time. I want it to be what you want, not what just I want." Layla took a deep breath. "And this isn't me being controlling either; it's making sure you're sure so we don't get hurt again.

"I've never wanted anyone like I want you. I understand we're going to fight, it's our nature but I never want us to go to bed at night angry with each other." He reached into his shirt pocket and pulled out an old velvet bag. "And your answer is?"

"I love you so much, Tyson. I want this to work."

"Trust me on this, because I know we can do it." He pulled the ring from the bag and held it in front of her face.

The tiny diamonds glimmered in the lamplight, the old-fashioned setting unique and very pretty.

"This is only tiny but it comes with a lot of love. Pa gave it to me to give to you if you'll have me. Seems he has more faith in us than we have in ourselves."

"It's adorable and perfect. I do love you, Tyson Watson. No matter how much we fight and how many times I have to bite my tongue and take back the words I spout out before I think, I'll always love you. The answer is yes."

THE END

If you enjoyed *Her Favorite Cowboy*, you'll love the next book in…

The Watson Brother series

Four Montana brothers searching for love…sometimes in the most unexpected circumstances.

Book 1: *Chance for Love*

Book 2: *The Sheriff's Mail-Order Bride*

Book 3: *The Doctor's Husband*

Book 4: *Her Favorite Cowboy*

Available now at your favorite online retailer!

About the Author

After moving to the lush green wine region of Australia's Hunter Valley, Ann has the perfect surrounding to let her imagination to run wild. She alternates her time between writing western romances, women's fiction romantic and playing in her garden.

Two kinds of hero make Ann to a mass of nerves. The hot cowboy with a slow sexy drawl (she used to live out in the desert and enjoyed every minute) and a man in a kilt. (Imagine Jamie Fraser) She can't wait to visit Scotland where she can get her fill of the tartan clad hotties for, um research purposes, of course.

In the meantime, her dear husband puts up with her talking to her characters and getting lost in worlds only she can imagine as she battles to bring stories to the page for everyone to enjoy.

Visit her website at AnnBHarrisonRomance.com

Thank you for reading

Her Favorite Cowboy

If you enjoyed this book, you can find more from all our great authors at TulePublishing.com, or from your favorite online retailer.

TULE
PUBLISHING